Silver Gulch Feud

It only takes a few hours for Yick Lee and Carter Lyle to realize that they've picked the wrong day to start working for Lorne Wayne. For the past two years Lorne has feuded with Alistair Marriott over the ownership of the Silver Gulch mine. But now the mine's giant protection man, Abe Mountain, is hell-bent on ripping apart that feud by blasting into oblivion anyone who stands in his way.

Lee and Carter face a desperate battle to uncover the buried truths about the mine. But can they succeed? And can Abe's guns be silenced? Only then can the Silver Gulch feud come to an end.

By the same author

Ambush in Dust Creek

Silver Gulch Feud

Scott Connor

© Scott Connor 2004
First published in Great Britain 2004

ISBN 0 7090 7537 5

Robert Hale Limited
Clerkenwell House
Clerkenwell Green
London EC1R 0HT

The right of Scott Connor to be identified as
author of this work has been asserted by him
in accordance with the Copyright, Designs and
Patents Act 1988.

Typeset by
Derek Doyle & Associates, Liverpool.
Printed and bound in Great Britain by
Antony Rowe Limited, Wiltshire

CHAPTER 1

With his shoulders slumped, Yick Lee stood on the boardwalk outside the town marshal's office.

Towards the end of another oppressively hot day in Silver Creek, the only sounds interrupting his torpor were the steady buzz of flies and the rattle of the heavy wagons trundling over unyielding rocky ground.

Two passing miners glanced at Lee, their heads cocked to one side. As soon as Lee nodded to them, they turned and scurried down the road.

Today, Lee had applied for seven jobs: two porters, one clerk, one foreman, and three waiters. Although Lee was available to start work immediately and each place had a desperate need, he remained unemployed.

Despite these setbacks, Lee forced himself to adopt the welcoming smile that he'd promised he'd present to the world, whatever the world presented to him, and moved towards the office door.

He arranged the blanket, his sole possession aside from his clothes, over his right shoulder, pushed the door open, and strode inside.

Marshal Brown sat behind his desk. For the barest fraction of a second he glanced up, noting Lee with a cold flash of his narrowed eyes. Then he stared at his desk, where he'd arranged playing-cards in a convoluted pattern.

Brown grabbed two cards and tapped them against his chin.

''Told you before,' he said, his voice low and bored. 'Go away.'

Lee gritted his teeth and shook his head. 'But I've never met you before, sir.'

Still keeping his head down, Brown yawned and gestured at the door with a casual wave.

'Still ain't interested. I don't get involved in your disputes. Sort it out on your own.'

Lee frowned. 'I've no dispute to bring to your attention, sir. I've come about your notice.'

Brown sighed long and hard. He threw down his cards and leaned back in his chair. With a long finger, he pushed his stetson back on his head and smiled. Although his cheeks creased around the lips, the eyes stayed cold.

'Let's have it. Which one of my wanted men have you seen? If the information is worth anything, I'll pay – after I have the man behind bars.'

Lee held his arms out and widened his smile.

'No, sir. I have no information on wanted men, yet. I mean your notice advertising for a deputy town marshal. I have come to apply.'

'You can't be serious,' Brown murmured with a pronounced gulp.

Lee edged forward a pace. 'I am. According to my sources, you have had no applicants, and your notice says that you'll decide at sunset tonight.'

Brown turned from his desk to stare through the window, a lopsided grin on his face.

'I'm sorry. You ain't what I'm looking for in a deputy.'

'And what are you looking for?'

Brown chewed his bottom lip and snorted.

Many others in Silver Creek had told Lee to his face what they were looking for – and put politely, that wasn't Lee. The only job the likes of Yick Lee could do were the invisible jobs – mining dangerous tunnels, shovelling excrement, and anything else that no one wanted to do.

But as Marshal Brown was a man of the law, Lee hoped that a nugget of decency rested in him.

'Look, Mr… What is your name?'

With a huge grin, Lee held out a hand.

'My name is Yick Lee – but I prefer Lee. Pleased to meet you, Marshal Brown.'

Brown glanced at the hand, then stared through the window again.

'Mr Lee, I want you to heed this. This is a tough mining town. The men who ride into Silver Creek come from the Silver Gulch mine, and they're as rough as you'll find anywhere. When they finish their shifts they want to unwind, and that calls for plenty of drinking and whoring and fighting. Things can get mighty rowdy.'

As he slipped his hand behind his back, Lee nodded.

'I know.'

'I need a man that can handle drunken behaviour, a man that can let hard-working miners unwind, but will stop them getting too violent.' Brown turned to Lee and pointed at him. 'Mr Lee, I ask you, is that man likely to be a … to be someone as short as you?'

Lee snorted. The American nationals prided themselves on working hard and playing hard, but in the mine they didn't work such long shifts as the Asian Americans and they didn't have such hard and cramped seams to dig as his people.

'I've worked down the mine,' he snapped, showing Brown his work-roughened hands. He set his squat legs wide. 'I'm tough enough.'

Brown frowned. 'I need a man who can ride well.'

Lee's grin returned in amazement that Brown was giving him a chance.

'That's me.'

Brown pointed at Lee's waist. 'You ain't packing a gun. Can you shoot well enough to fight off the sort of troublemakers we get in Silver Creek?'

'I owned a gun before I was a miner. I'm a good shot.'

With his frown deepening, Brown turned to stare out of the window.

'I don't know,' he murmured.

'Give me a chance. That's all I ask. I won't disappoint you.'

For long moments, Brown tapped his chin. Then, with a sigh, he shuffled round on his chair and stared at his playing-cards. He moved a card an inch to the right.

'I'll think on it, when all the applications are in.'
'I'll wait.'
'Yeah,' Brown mumbled, then slid another card to the side and rested his chin on an upturned hand.

Lee pointed at the door. 'I'll do my waiting outside, if that's all right?'

With a cough, Brown lowered his head to stare even more intently at his cards.

Lee wandered outside and leaned on the wall, then slid back down to sit on the boardwalk by the door. He slipped his blanket under him and shuffled down, seeking some comfort on the hard wood.

From out of the cloudless sky the sun blasted down. Lee yawned and closed his eyes.

Although he wanted to stay awake, he hadn't eaten that day and within seconds, his eyelids became heavy.

He rested his chin on his knees and closed his eyes.

A timeless period later, a blast of gunfire from outside the Hot Silver Saloon awoke Lee. He stretched and yawned.

It was twilight, the first tendrils of the evening chill slipping under his blanket.

With a last huge yawn, Lee pushed to his feet. He wrapped his blanket around his shoulders and shuffled into the marshal's office.

Inside, Brown was pottering around. He moved a rifle from one locker to another, then moved it back.

For a full minute Lee watched him. He coughed, but Brown then glared intently at his display of Wanted posters.

'It is after sunset, Marshal Brown,' Lee said. 'I have returned to hear your decision.

For a long time, Brown continued to glare at the posters, then he hung his head. He shook it, sighing, then turned to Lee. In his left hand he cradled his right elbow, and lifted his right hand to hold his chin.

'Mr . . . Mr . . .'

'Lee.'

Brown nodded and rubbed his chin. 'Mr Lee, I have a problem with employing you and I'd be dishonest if I didn't tell you the truth.'

'Go on.'

Brown sighed and glanced around his office, looking at anything but Lee, then, finally, his cold gaze settled on him.

'I have no problem with you, but many people in Silver Creek will have. Seeing a Chinese man with a deputy's badge will cause trouble. People will pick fights with you, and the role of the law is to reduce trouble, not to generate it.'

'The danger is to me, and I don't shy from trouble.'

With a harsh chuckle, Brown smiled.

'You'd get plenty of practice. Trouble would find you, pretty darn fast.'

'Maybe I will attract trouble. But I say I can handle myself and I can prove it. I can only do that if you give me the chance.'

Brown shook his head. 'My answer is still no.'

Lee turned, his head hanging, his shoulders slumped from more than just fatigue. He shuffled two paces towards the door, then smiled to himself and stopped. He turned back and considered Brown a moment, then edged forward a short pace. He cocked his head to one side.

'Have any other applicants come forward?'

Brown winced and hung his head.

Lee bit his bottom lip as he fought to suppress the faint hope that hit him and threatened to blossom.

Brown looked up and rocked his head from side to side.

Then Lee smelled something stale. He turned.

A grimed and hulking cowhand stood in the doorway. Beneath the grime, the cowhand was young-faced, but thick-set, and from the dust coating his threadbare clothes, he looked as though he'd been on the trail for many weeks.

Brown glanced at the cowhand. 'And who are you?'

'Name's Carter, Carter Lyle, sir.'

'And what can I do for you, Carter?'

'Would you be the marshal of this here town?' Carter asked.

'I am.'

With a gleaming smile, Carter whistled through his teeth.

'Then this sure is my lucky day. I heard that you is looking for a deputy.'

Lee sighed. As he expected, a grin spread across Brown's face.

Brown turned to Lee, his eyes gleaming.

'Looks like I have two applicants now, but only one job.'

'You be the other applicant?' Carter asked, turning to Lee.

'Yup,' Lee muttered.

Carter held out his right, dirt-streaked hand.

'Then I wish you luck, and I got no hard feelings if you're the better man.'

Despite his irritation, Lee took the offered hand and introduced himself while Carter shook the hand in his firm grip.

Brown rubbed his hands. 'So, Carter, tell me about yourself. You look like a man with plenty of hard riding experience.'

Carter shuffled a scuffed boot in a circle, creating a grimy swathe across the floor.

'No,' he murmured. 'Back on our farm, we couldn't afford horses, so I don't have much experience of hard riding. I mainly hid on freight trains and walked here.'

Brown coughed. 'Most that goes on around here doesn't involve riding. Trouble arrives in town without asking, but you look like you're a man who can take care of himself. How good a shot do you fancy yourself to be?'

Carter added another grimy swathe to the floor with his other boot.

'Sorry, Mr Marshal. I've never owned a gun. Back on our farm, we couldn't afford guns.'

Brown coughed again. 'I reckon too many lawmen overrate gunfighting skills. I like my deputies to keep their guns holstered and not to react without thinking. So, how are you in a fist-fight? Unless you couldn't afford them back on your farm.'

Carter grinned and smashed a fist into his other hand, producing a puff of dust.

'We sure could have fights. And I used to fair whup my brother when he got too ornery.'

While smiling, Brown rubbed his hands and nodded to Lee.

'That's what I wanted to hear.'

Carter widened the swathe of grime on the floor.

'Excepting my brother is only ten years old.'

With a sigh, Brown rubbed his sweating forehead.

'My notice asked for tough, dependable men to apply for the deputy's job.'

Frowning, Carter shuffled from side to side.

'Did it? I can't do reading. We couldn't afford fancy books on my farm.'

Brown sighed deeply and muttered to himself.

'Marshal,' Lee said, striding forward a pace, 'with all due respect to my fellow applicant, who can't ride, shoot, fight or read, I reckon you've heard our qualifications for the job. So, which one of us are you picking for your deputy?'

Brown hung his head a moment. Then he looked up and glared at Lee, his eyes cold.

'Do you need to ask?'

CHAPTER 2

Captain Nathan McPherson stood to attention as Sergeant Parish marched towards him across the dusty corral.

Parish slammed his feet together, coming to attention crisply. But he stared over Nathan's left shoulder, avoiding his eyes.

'Captain,' Parish said in brisk, military tones while saluting, 'what are your orders?'

With a returning salute, Nathan gritted his teeth.

'By the order of Mayor Hains, on this day, 7 April 1875, we are to execute Clam Maxwell, Jack Town and Abe Mountain for gunrunning. Their deaths by firing squad.'

Parish saluted. He swivelled on his heel and marched to the side.

Nathan took a deep breath and turned to face the prisoners.

Ten miles out of Fort Riley in a windswept corral, the three prisoners stood. Thick ropes bound their arms and legs to firing-posts. Their chests were bared for the bullets that would end their lives.

Nathan marched ten yards to stand before the first prisoner.

'Clam Maxwell,' he said, 'do you have any last words?'

With wide protruding eyes, Clam glared back. His grime-lined face masked the patchwork of scars his lengthy career had earned him. Clam spat on the ground, then licked his lips and turned from Nathan to stare at the open plains, his chin held aloft.

In relief that Clam hadn't spat at him, Nathan nodded.

'All right, no last words. Do you want the blindfold?'

Clam glared back at Nathan and sneered, revealing a wide expanse of yellow teeth. Then with the barest movement, Clam nodded.

Nathan waved for Parish to complete his request, then marched to the next prisoner.

'Jack Town, do you have any last words?'

Jack snuffled and rubbed his dribbling nose on his shoulder. The effort didn't stop the wetness running over his mouth. He relented from his futile efforts and glared back.

'No point,' he mumbled between wheezes. 'Don't think you'll want to hear from the likes of me.'

Nathan shook his head. 'You're wrong. A condemned man can say whatever he wants to say.'

So Jack did.

Despite hearing several choice and physically impossible actions Nathan could do to himself, which he noted for future use on errant recruits, Nathan maintained a fixed smile.

When a burst of violent coughing ended Jack's tirade, Nathan nodded.

'Thank you kindly. Do you want the blindfold?'

Jack spat on the ground and glared at Nathan, then his shoulders slumped and he nodded.

As Parish blindfolded Jack, Nathan marched to the last prisoner.

Although Nathan was of average height, he stared at the centre of Abe's chest. Even though Mountain was tied, with three times the bonds of the other well-secured prisoners, a flurry of alarm shook in the pit of Nathan's stomach while he was within this man's substantial reach.

Two weeks ago, they'd captured Abe. They'd used twelve men to hold him down. Afterwards, every man had bruises from head to foot and they'd regretted that they hadn't brought more men.

To preserve dignity, Nathan stepped back. Three paces from the prisoner, he rocked back on his heels to see Abe's face.

'Abe Mountain, do you have any last words?'

Although his voice was robust enough to scream orders across a fort, whenever Nathan spoke to Abe his voice sounded light and airy. He felt as if he were talking to a giant redwood.

Abe stared over Nathan's head, his gaze elsewhere.

Just as Nathan decided that Abe wouldn't acknowledge him, his vast, bristling red beard and shaggy shock of hair dropped down. Inch by inch the head descended until the piercing blue eyes were on him.

Nathan smiled – he'd discovered something about Abe. Whenever possible, he acted slowly to lull people into thinking he always moved slowly. This trick must have fooled many people. They would later discover that when he wanted to, Abe could move with a speed that defied belief.

'I have something to say,' Abe boomed. 'I'm holding you responsible for my arrest. You'll regret your actions, as will everyone who ever crossed me. The time has come to right wrongs.'

Nathan nodded. He'd received the three standard forms of last words when prisoners faced death: surly silence, abuse, and threats.

'Thank you for the warning. Do you want the blindfold?'

Abe lifted his piercing gaze from Nathan and stared over his head, across the barren wilderness.

'When death catches me, it'll have to sneak up on me when my eyes are closed or I ain't looking. Otherwise it couldn't get the better of me.'

'All right,' Nathan said. Many prisoners couldn't admit they needed help at the end. This obtuse way of asking for a blindfold wasn't unusual. He gestured to Parish to bring the blindfold.

Abe chuckled, the sound like boulders thundering in a landslide.

'So I won't need the blindfold. Death won't catch *me* today. Not when I can look straight at it.'

Nathan shrugged. He came to attention, marched to the side and did an abrupt right turn.

'Burial duty,' he shouted, 'report at the double.'

The burial duty quick marched into the corral, dragging behind them the burial cart on which they'd move the dead men. They stood beside the line of firing-posts and to Nathan's orders, removed their hats and stood at ease with their heads bowed.

Nathan marched ten paces, did another right turn, then marched until he stood beside his firing duty.

Nathan counted to ten.

'Firing duty,' he roared, 'present arms.'

Rifles and hands clapped together.

'Ready,' Parish shouted.

Nathan shared salutes with Parish, unsheathed his sword, and lifted it high above his head.

'Firing duty, take aim.'

His firing duty thrust one leg forward and swung their rifles up, aiming two at each prisoner.

'All ready,' Parish shouted.

'Firing duty—'

One man screeched and staggered back a pace, breaking the line.

Nathan advanced a long pace to command him to get back in line, but then the rest of the men staggered back a pace, too.

A deep crunching sounded behind Nathan. He swirled round.

Abe had stood and with his huge legs set wide, he'd ripped the firing-post from the ground.

Nathan tried to order his men to fire, but his own surprise paralysed his throat a moment and he just croaked indistinctly while he waved his sword in a vague circle.

With the post still attached to his back, Abe bent over and swung it in an arc, scything through the equally surprised burial duty. When the post splintered in two over the third man's head, Abe threw it away, ripping away his bonds in a shower of rope. Then, with a lunge of his thick arm, he hit the last member of the burial duty in the stomach.

The man flew backward to wind around Jack's firing-post.

As if seeing this was the final proof Nathan needed that this wasn't a nightmare, he screamed at his firing duty to open fire.

The men took aim, then lowered their guns, then took aim again.

'Fire,' Nathan screeched again.

'We might hit our own men,' Parish yelled.

'Just do it!'

Rifles swung towards Abe and gunfire ripped across the corral, arcing through the two prisoners who were still tied to their posts, but when the gunfire reached Abe, Abe hurled himself behind the burial cart.

The firing duty knelt and trained their guns on the cart, waiting for Abe to emerge, but two great clawing hams of hands appeared from behind the cart and dragged two of the pole-axed burial duty away.

Abe tossed the men on to their fronts and when he leapt to his feet, he had a gun in both hands.

Gunshots exploded across the corral.

In a ripple of sudden movement, Parish and the firing duty stumbled back with their chests pitted red.

Then Abe swung round to Nathan.

Nathan cried out as a gunshot ripped the sword from his hand.

The gunshots echoed away to nothing, leaving the body-strewn corral shrouded in eerie quiet.

While Abe hurled the cart aside and stormed towards him, Nathan fell to his knees and scrambled for one of his men's rifles. His hand slapped on a weapon, but pain sliced through his hand. The gunshot, which had torn his sword away, had ripped clean through his palm. He tried to force his shaking fingers around the rifle, but his fingers wouldn't move.

Then a vast shadow blotted out the sun.

Nathan stared up at Abe, who loomed over him, his guns held high, a smile breaking his great shaggy beard.

'Like I promised,' Abe boomed, 'death will need to catch me unawares. And your men were nowhere near sneaky enough.'

'You promised to hold *me* responsible for your arrest,' Nathan babbled. 'You had no reason to kill my men.'

The sound of boulders crunching filled Nathan's mind as Abe chuckled.

'I'll take those for your last words. Do you want a blindfold?'

Nathan shook his head and Abe's two guns swung towards him.

CHAPTER 3

In the Hot Silver Saloon, Yick Lee slipped on to a stool at the end of the bar.

Rough-clad miners, who'd spent half their lives underground, and smartly dressed men, who'd never soiled their hands in their lives, filled the saloon.

The noise was only at the level of excited chatter. This early in the evening, the bulk of the miners had yet to arrive, so the raucous singing and fighting hadn't begun.

With his failure to get the deputy's job, Lee had been ready to slope out of Silver Creek and start the long journey back to the Pacific Ocean, perhaps followed by an even longer journey.

But Carter had insisted he stay for a drink.

As the nights in Silver Creek produced a bone-aching cold that his blanket couldn't repel, Lee had relented.

'Are you sure that you want to be in here with me?' Lee asked.

Carter kicked the counter, his shoulders hunched. 'Why not? I'm as big a failure as you are. We both ain't suitable deputy material.'

'That's as maybe, but they won't serve me. This saloon wouldn't give me work earlier.'

With his head on one side, Carter bunched his eyebrows.

'I don't see why they wouldn't give you work. Back on my farm, my pa never turned away any man who wanted work.' Carter sighed. 'Mind you, he turned away plenty who wanted paid.'

'Life is different in Silver Creek – not everyone prospers.'

Carter waved, attracting the bartender's attention.

As the bartender strolled down the bar towards Carter, Lee shuffled off his stool. He backed two strides and turned to watch the bartender's and Carter's reflections in the saloon window.

Carter and the bartender shared low words, but to Lee's irritation, the bartender waved his towel at them, then pointed to the door.

Carter joined Lee and stood hunched.

Lee matched Carter's posture. 'Wouldn't serve you, then?'

Carter shook his head. 'Nope.'

'As I expected,' Lee snapped. 'The townsfolk will never accept me.'

'He didn't mention you. He just reckoned that having no money was a problem.'

'How did you hope to get drinks?' Lee spluttered.

Carter frowned, his jaw set in earnest surprise that the bartender hadn't given him free drinks. He shuffled inside his soiled buckskin jacket.

'I've learned one thing in life: if you don't ask, you

don't find out anything. If you ask and get nowhere, you ain't lost anything.'

Lee glanced at Carter's ragged clothing, all covered in varying types of dirt.

'Asking is fine, but failing every time can destroy you.'

Carter hunched his wide shoulders and pointed across the saloon.

'Then follow me. I'll show you what worked for me earlier.'

Shaking his head, Lee followed Carter across the crowded saloon.

At the side of the saloon, Carter approached a stetson-wearing man, Silas Malt. Carter slipped his tattered hat from his head and held it across his chest. He smiled.

'Sir,' he said, 'I want to thank you for directing me towards that job working as a deputy, but the marshal didn't want to hire me or my friend.'

'Pity, friend,' Silas said, without turning from his fellow drinker.

'Do you know of any other suitable jobs?'

Silas sighed. He glanced at Lee, then turned to Carter.

'No, but you might want to join your friend down the mine. If you're not interested in that, I'll tell you if I hear of anything else.'

With studied finality, Silas turned his back on Carter.

Carter pointed to a gap in the milling drinkers and led Lee to the wall, where he leaned back and set his feet wide. With his shoulders hunched, he faced the bustling saloon folk.

Lee copied the posture. 'So, what are we waiting for?'

'We're waiting to see someone who might give us a job, or a drink.'

'I'd settle for either.'

Carter frowned. 'Was that man right? Do you work in the mine?'

'I did work down the Silver Gulch mine,' Lee snapped.

'Then you should stay there. This search for work could take some time.'

'I ain't. I worked there for two years.' Lee coughed and kneaded his brow as he forced himself to speak. 'But four months ago, a tunnel collapsed and trapped twenty-seven miners. They all died.'

Carter gulped. 'I'm sorry. I didn't know.'

'The trapped people included my brother and just about everyone I've ever known.' Lee chuckled without humour. 'The ridiculous thing is, for the previous year a dispute about pay had rumbled on. But after the disaster, nobody worried about the money, just the conditions. So they boarded up the dangerous tunnels and everything carried on as if nothing had happened.'

'And you ain't returned since?

'I returned,' Lee muttered, trying to keep the bitterness from his voice, but knowing that he was failing. 'I had to eat, but today I've had enough of the grime and the dust and the filth. So, here I am on the outside, without work. But I ain't returning.'

'I came to Silver Creek because I heard it was as

prosperous as Silver Town is. Perhaps I heard wrong.' Carter sighed and leaned against the wall. 'From the sound of your experiences here, the likes of us won't prosper.'

'Maybe for you, Silver Creek will be fine, but for me and. . .' Lee fingered a frayed end of his blanket. 'Let's just say that I came east searching for a better life. I didn't expect to find this.'

Carter chuckled and Lee glared at him.

Carter shook his head. 'I ain't laughing at you. It's odd that everyone I know went west to search for a better life, yet you went east.'

Lee shrugged. 'Depends on where you started.'

For twenty minutes they stood in silence. Then Silas wandered over to them.

'I've heard about work you boys might be interested in,' he said, patting each man on the shoulder.

Carter pushed himself from the wall. 'Tell us. We'll do anything.'

'I wouldn't say that too loudly. There are plenty of lonely miners around.' Silas smirked, then pointed outside. 'But if you head to Lorne Wayne's ranch, he's looking for workers.'

Lee snorted. Lorne Wayne was one of the mine owners.

'Thought so,' he snapped. 'I might have known the only work around here for me was down the mine.'

'That's where you're wrong. Lorne wants ranch hands. Just see the ranch boss, Stem Buckfast.'

'Thanks,' Carter said.

Silas shrugged. 'There's no need to thank me.

Pay's no good. The work can be hard and nobody wants to do it, but I told you I'd let you know if I heard anything.'

Carter glanced at Lee, but Lee nodded.

'Thank you kindly,' Lee said. 'The job sounds excellent. We'll try first thing tomorrow.'

Lee tipped his hat and Silas waddled away.

'Are you sure the work sounds excellent?' Carter asked. 'The work is hard and the pay is poor.'

'Nope.' Lee pushed from the wall and smiled. 'The man said the magic words that told me the work is perfect for us.'

Carter furrowed his brow. 'What's that?'

'No one wants to do it, and let's face facts.' Lee patted Carter on the back. 'That's the only work we'll get.'

CHAPTER 4

Jeremy Montana stared through the window of his second-floor office in Bear Rock, watching the carts and the horses bustle back and forth on the main road. He yawned, then sat back and stretched in his padded chair.

The afternoon had the right level of heat and lack of clients that Jeremy loved. And now he was anticipating a lengthy siesta for the rest of the afternoon.

As he locked his hands behind his head and crossed his legs on the desk, his secretary, Martha, pushed open his office door.

'You have a visitor, Mr Montana,' she said. 'Shall I show him in?'

'No,' Jeremy murmured through a long yawn.

Martha leaned on the door frame and glanced back down the corridor. She shivered, then glared at Jeremy.

'Mr Montana,' she said, lowering her voice, 'he's waiting to see you. Shall I show him in?'

With the siesta receding fast, Jeremy rolled his feet to the floor and gave Martha a curt nod.

'All right. All right. Show him in, but he's the last one I'll see today.'

Martha nodded and turned from the doorway. She backed to press herself against the corridor wall and stared towards the ceiling.

Jeremy flinched as his visitor strode to the doorway. From beneath the lintel, Jeremy saw only his body up to his densely bearded chin.

In an exaggerated style, the man ducked to his waist to shuffle into Jeremy's office. Once inside, he drew to his full height. The man didn't wear a hat. If he did, Jeremy reckoned it would probably brush against the ceiling.

'Mr Jones is a new client,' Martha said from the corridor.

'You don't say.' Jeremy forced a smile. 'Sit down, Mr Jones.'

Mr Jones sat in the only available chair by striding over it and dropping on to it. The chair groaned.

'Thank you kindly.' Mr Jones's booming voice rattled the ornaments on Jeremy's side cabinet.

Jeremy pushed a document aside to clear a space in the centre of his desk, clasped his hands, and leaned forward. Then, finding that he stared up at Mr Jones, he leaned back to avoid the inevitable neck strain.

'So, Mr Jones, what can I do for you?'

'I want to review a contract that you produced eighteen months ago for some of my colleagues.'

Jeremy unclasped his hands and held them wide.

'And you'd like me to produce something similar for you?'

'You have the general idea.' Mr Jones set his untamed red beard in the centre of his chest.

'I can't show you the specific contract that I produced for your colleagues – client confidentiality and all that – but if you give me their names, I'll talk you through the particulars of their contract.'

With his piercing blue eyes fixed on Jeremy, Mr Jones ground his teeth.

'They were Alistair Marriott and Lorne Wayne. The contract was for mineral rights.'

With a small mystery solved, Jeremy smiled. Mr Jones didn't seem to be someone who'd have trouble enforcing his rights, but mineral ownership was something everyone needed help to clarify.

'Understood. I can't remember the specific case, but most mineral contracts have similar clauses. I can run through the terms and explain the main problem areas.'

Mr Jones leaned forward and slammed an elbow on the desk. The desk creaked and swayed. Mr Jones widened his eyes, his blue eyes so piercing that Jeremy gulped and leaned further back in his chair so that the back of his head thumped against the wall.

'I was more interested in their specific contract.'

'Perhaps in this circumstance.' Jeremy's voice shook with an uncontrolled tremor and he coughed to regain his composure. 'I can take you through the specific terms in their contract.'

Jeremy bounded from his desk to his filing cupboard.

Even without Martha's help, he quickly located the

file kept under the name of Lorne Wayne. With a folder of documents tucked under his arm, he scurried back to his desk and slid out the bound contracts.

Jeremy rummaged through his paperwork. As he read his notes, he recalled the complexities that had taken up two days' work and two weeks' billed time, some months ago.

'This is more difficult than I first thought. Do you want to see the first contract or the two later contracts?'

Mr Jones leaned his other elbow on Jeremy's desk. The desk creaked with increasing danger.

'All of them.'

To avoid looking at Mr Jones more than he had to, Jeremy leaned over his papers and examined the first contract.

'Apparently the Silver Gulch mine was under the junction of land owned by the two men we mentioned, so the first contract split the rights to the mine between them.' Jeremy glanced at the second contract. The terms were identical to the first, except for the people involved. 'The second contract allocated rights to a third man, a Mr Mountain.'

Mr Jones leaned forward, the desk creaking some more.

'And the final contract?'

Jeremy glanced at the third contract. 'That contract excluded Mr Mountain from those rights and replaced them with rights for a new man, a Marshal Brown.'

With an explosive sigh, Mr Jones leaned back in

his chair. The desk rocked from him. The documents fluttered to the floor.

'I didn't know that. How could they exclude Abe Mountain?'

Jeremy rescued his notes from the floor and shuffled through them to refresh his memory.

'Simple, Mr Wayne and Mr Marriott always retained the right to change the contract whenever they both agreed to do so. Not that it matters. Three months ago Mr Mountain died. I have the notice of death here signed by Marshal Brown.'

Mr Jones nodded, his vast head shaking the unkempt beard against his chest.

'So, Mr Mountain has no rights to the mine, in any circumstances?'

Jeremy saw a hint of what Mr Jones wanted.

'No. Mr Mountain's estate doesn't have rights. If you're a relative of the deceased man, I'm sorry to tell you that the original contract is no longer valid. However valuable those rights may be.'

With a beaming smile, Mr Jones leaned forward and stabbed a thick finger on the contract.

'Understood. In that case, you'll produce a new contract for me.'

Jeremy sighed in relief and relaxed his shoulders.

'And the new contract will use the same types of terms and clauses as this final contract?'

Mr Jones pushed the contract to Jeremy.

'Exactly the same, except for one final clause.'

'Which is?'

With his gaze fixed downward on Jeremy, Mr Jones grabbed either side of the desk in two huge hands.

'I'll add the final clause myself, once you've drawn up the rest of the contract.'

Jeremy sighed, wondering whether to complain about the problems that always occurred whenever a non-lawyer amended a contract, but he shrugged and grabbed his pen, ready to take notes.

'And the names of the persons I should include in the contract?'

Mr Jones's smile widened, splitting his red beard and moustache with two rows of gleaming white teeth.

'Like I said, I want the contract to be identical to the final contract for ownership of the Silver Gulch mine. Same names, same mine, same everything, except for the final clause.'

Gulping, Jeremy examined the notes on his desk.

'But why? Such a contract has no worth.'

'Because I want it,' Mr Jones roared.

From sitting so close to such a loud explosion of noise, Jeremy's head rattled.

As he shook his head to free the ringing that filled his ears, he thought of a dozen reasons why he shouldn't produce a copy of the contract, and only one reason why he should. As the reason he should was sitting in his office, and filling most of it, he nodded.

Normally, he'd tell a new client to collect the finished work in a week, to preserve the mystery that his job was complex, but today he grabbed his pen and a clean sheet of paper.

'Give me fifteen minutes.'

Mr Jones gripped the desk more tightly. Splinters broke off the sides.

'You have five.'

Jeremy gulped. 'Five it is.'

Working quickly, Jeremy kept his head down from Mr Jones's gaze and copied the contract. With the writing complete, he dated, embossed and sealed the contract.

As Jeremy blew on the wax to set it, with a clawing ham of a hand Mr Jones ripped the contract from Jeremy's fingers. In Mr Jones's hand the contract looked like a tissue. He glanced at it and smiled.

'This is a good piece of work.'

Mr Jones slotted the contract into an inside pocket, then grabbed the original contract from the desk. With a quick gesture, he shredded the contract, the pieces falling through his thick fingers to the floor.

As with all his contracts, Jeremy had filed a copy in the mayor's office, but his heart still beat faster.

'If you think that you have the valid contract, it's still the same as—'

'I know that.' Mr Jones batted the shreds of the original contract from his jacket. He stood and loomed over Jeremy. 'But I intend to renegotiate.'

Jeremy held his arms wide. 'I can help you do that.'

'Just like you helped sign away Abe Mountain's rights, I suppose?' Mr Jones snorted. 'I don't need the kind of help worms like you provide.'

Mr Jones lunged over the desk and grabbed Jeremy's throat. With one great hand, he lifted him off the floor.

Jeremy batted his fists against Mr Jones's hand, but

the fingers were like iron.

'You ain't Mr Jones,' he gasped. 'You're Abe Mountain.'

'Got it in one.'

Jeremy heard something crack. A dull ache spread from his neck to fill his whole body and his long-awaited siesta dragged him into darkness.

CHAPTER 5

Two hours before sunrise, Lee and Carter walked out of Silver Creek.

Although the trail to Lorne Wayne's ranch was hard and well travelled, nobody passed them by as they trudged along.

The sun inched above the horizon and within minutes it blasted away the chill dawn breeze. By the time they staggered to a trading post, both men's clothes were sweat-drenched and sticking to their bowed backs.

According to the directions they'd received, the trading post marked the half-way point between Silver Creek and Lorne Wayne's ranch.

Other trails crossed this point. One trail led to Alistair Marriott's ranch. The widest trail to the Silver Gulch mine.

Lee pointedly turned his back on the mine route.

Both men glanced at the trading post and licked their lips, but without funds, they had no choice other than to continue trudging.

The sun was high and beating down relentless

heat on the barren land when they staggered to the fence, which marked the edge of the Wayne ranch.

At the ranch gates, they looked over the ranch house and outbuildings.

The riches Lorne Wayne must have gained from the mine ought to be significant, yet the ranch buildings were rough-built and crumbling. Horseless corrals festered untended. Equipment was dust-coated and rusty.

A handful of yawning ranch hands slouched against mouldering fence posts. The men were unshaven and unwashed, and dressed in dusty clothes grimed from inactivity instead of hard work.

While Lee and Carter stood by the unguarded gate, the only thing that seemed to be happening was a ranch hand whittling a stick.

Lee and Carter shared a shrug, then edged past the open gate.

The stocky ranch boss, Stem, glanced at them. He yawned, pushed from his post, and sauntered two paces closer, then slouched to a halt.

Lee and Carter strode towards him and halted. Both men stood tall.

'Howdy,' Lee shouted. 'You be Stem Buckfast?'

'Yup.' Stem spat a long brown stream of tobacco drool to the side. He scratched his wide paunch, then tipped back his hat to run a hand through his greying hair. 'What can I do for you?'

'We hear that you're hiring.'

'Might be.'

Lee gulped down a flurry of hope. 'We're hard-working, skilled in most things you need, and available to start right away.'

Stem ran his tongue over his lips as he looked them up and down.

'If you two is so highly skilled, why ain't you applying to work at the Marriott ranch? Elliott Jameson pays twice what I'm prepared to pay.'

'Twice the rate?' Carter spluttered. He cupped a hand over his mouth and turned to Lee. 'Why are we here, Lee?'

Lee snorted and stared at Carter until he nodded back. Lee didn't need to say that a ranch boss paying twice the going rate wouldn't be looking for the likes of them.

He glanced around the ranch, lingering his gaze on the sparse trampled vegetation, the badly boarded stable, the broken fences. Then he turned back to Stem.

'We're here because we wanted to come here.'

Stem shook his head. 'No one wants to come here any more, except for the desperate and the incompetent. Which are you?'

'We're available.'

Stem nodded. A real smile broke his weather-lined face.

'You still have your pride, then. But why should I employ an ex-miner who's had enough of standing knee-deep in everyone's filth and a farm boy who's run away from home?'

Lee smiled. 'Because such people can work hard.'

Stem sighed and ran a grimed hand down his equally grimy jacket.

'I believe you, but you'll need to prove your worth.

Work for one month on half-pay and if you impress me, you're on full pay.'

Lee glared at Stem. This sounded like a worse rate of pay than the work he'd left.

Carter grabbed Lee's elbow and dragged him back a pace.

'Lee,' Carter whispered. 'He's taking advantage.'

'I know,' Lee whispered. 'But half-pay with the promise of full pay is better than no pay.'

Lee faced Stem and nodded.

Stem extended a grimed hand. 'Ignore what Lorne Wayne says. This is my ranch and you answer to me.'

Lee took the hand and stepped back for Carter to shake Stem's hand.

'You won't regret it,' Carter said.

Stem tipped his hat. ''Make sure I don't.'

As Stem turned to the stables, Carter leaned to Lee.

'Are you sure about this? He could pay us the half-pay, then fire us after a month.'

'You're right, but we need to make damn sure that we're so impressive, he won't dare fire us.'

'Really?' Carter smirked and Lee smiled back.

'Perhaps we won't be *that* impressive, but look at it this way. Stem will feed us for a month and, with luck, we can teach you how to ride a horse, fire a gun and a lot more besides.'

Carter nodded. 'So when we reach the next town, we *can* be impressive.'

In Hard Gully, the nearest town to Silver Creek, Abe

Mountain sauntered into the Lucky Dip Saloon and to the bar.

'What you want?' the bartender asked, blinking wildly as he appraised Abe.

By way of an answer, Abe just smiled and pointed at the two men, Rufus Tourney and Dale Miles, who were nursing their whiskies at the end of the bar. He sauntered to their side until his shadow fell over them.

'Abe,' Rufus murmured, looking up and staggering back a pace.

Abe's smile split his voluminous beard. 'Yup.'

'But—'

'Yeah, I know.' Abe barged between the two men and slammed a hand on each of their shoulders, which buckled them to their knees. 'You thought I was dead.'

Rufus righted himself and returned a slap to Abe's arm.

'Should have known they can't kill off your sort. Where have you been?'

'Been lying low for a while.'

Rufus laughed and backed a pace to look Abe up and down.

'Man your size must find it hard to lie low.'

Abe chuckled. 'And I guess you've been lying low for a while, too.'

Rufus glanced at Dale and both men snorted, then knocked back their whiskies.

'Had no choice. After Lorne and Alistair said that you'd died, Marshal Brown ran us out of town.'

'Heard Marshal Brown's name just once too often.

You ready to return to Silver Creek?'

Dale nodded. 'Sure am.'

Rufus nodded, too. 'As long as we can pay that marshal a visit.'

Abe dragged Rufus and Dale round, then hunched down.

'We will,' Abe said in low rumbling voice, which was his attempt at a whisper. 'Along with those mine owners.'

The three men grunted their agreement, rolled their shoulders, and headed for the door.

Outside, Dale turned to Abe.

'When we've disposed of them, what are you doing then?'

'I got me a contract.' Abe reached into his pocket and extracted the contract he'd obtained from Jeremy Montana. He unfolded it and held it out to Dale.

Dale took the contract and read it. His eyes narrowed.

'What's this you've added?' Dale muttered, stabbing a firm finger on the final clause.

Abe slammed his hands on his hips.

'You got a problem with it?'

'I sure have,' Dale waved the contract at Abe. 'It—'

Abe grabbed Dale's throat, cutting off his speech, and lifted him off the ground.

'What were you saying?'

Dale opened and closed his mouth soundlessly. The contract slipped from his dangling fingers. Then Abe hurled him at the horse rail. Dale crashed through it to smash against the saloon wall. His head slumped against his chest.

Abe turned to see that Rufus had grabbed the contract and was reading it.

Abe smiled. 'And have *you* got a problem with it?'

Rufus gulped. He glanced at the comatose Dale, then turned to face Abe. He shook his head.

'I reckon I understand. Whatever you're planning is fine with me.'

Rufus held out the contract for Abe to swipe it from his hand.

Abe chuckled. 'I had a feeling you might think like that.'

CHAPTER 6

Two hours into their new employment, Lee and Carter rode at the back of a line of ranch hands, heading towards Silver Creek.

Stem hadn't ordered them to clean out the stable, as Lee expected. Instead, he'd told them to pump water from the well for everyone, a duty that had taken far longer than they expected as they fought a seemingly endless battle to satisfy the other ranch hands' demands.

After that, Stem had told them to follow everyone else from the ranch.

Turning from the dusty trail, Lee glanced at Carter, who, although riding stiffly, wasn't faring as badly as Lee thought he might.

'I thought that you'd never ridden a horse?' Lee asked.

Carter shook his head. 'I said my family couldn't afford to buy horses on our farm. That don't mean I didn't get to ride horses from other farms.'

'Remind me to explain to you how you answer a potential employer's questions.'

'My pa always said I should tell the truth, so when Marshal Brown asked me if I had experience of hard riding, I told him I ain't.'

'My pa told me to tell the truth, too. It did me no good.'

After ten minutes of slow riding, Stem halted the cortège outside the trading post.

The sun was past its highest, the fierce glare from the light rock creating shimmering eddies across the barren landscape. To shelter his eyes, Lee held his hand to his brow as he watched everyone dismount.

As the ranch hands filed into the trading post, he and Carter dismounted, too.

With a shrug to Carter, Lee shuffled to stand behind the last man, Dave Trent.

'We here to get supplies?' he asked.

'Nope,' Dave said. 'We is getting out of the sun and getting into some entertainment. There be precious little to be had in here, but better than you'll get at the ranch.'

'But ain't we got more important things to do at the ranch?'

Dave glanced along the trails, which were empty for miles in all directions. He shrugged.

'Nope.'

The man queuing before him, Mitchell O'Flaherty, turned and laughed at Dave's comment and with that, they sauntered into the trading post.

Lee gulped back his irritation and marched inside after them.

The trading post provided everything that anyone could need. Food bags, clothing and prospecting tools filled the room in huge, teetering piles.

The ranch hands shuffled through a gap in the wares.

On the other side of the clutter there was a half-stable, half-smithy. By the back wall, a dozen beer barrels were dotted around a rough-hewn slab of wood set atop two barrels.

As soon as Lee and Carter emerged from the maze of supplies, Stem spun round and grinned at them.

'What do you boys fancy, then? Beer, beer, beer or beer?'

Lee smiled. 'Beer.'

Everyone burst into laughter, and the men's backs resounded to the sound of half a dozen well-aimed slaps.

With an arm wrapped around Lee's neck and his other arm wrapped around Carter's shoulders, Stem dragged them to the rough table where an apron-clad man stood, grinning.

'My young friend here would like a beer, and so would this one, and so would I.' Stem released his grip and spread his thick arms wide. 'And so would all of us.'

'Coming right up, Stem,' the bartender said. He poured a steady stream of beer into large unwashed tin mugs, the beer consisting of more foam than brew.

Stem threw a handful of coins on the table and leaned towards the bartender.

'Did you hear who's working at the Marriott ranch now?' he asked.

Lee tried to listen to the bartender's reply, but Carter leaned to him.

'Lee, this beer-drinking, is it all right?'

Lee turned to Carter. 'You have drunk beer before, haven't you?'

Carter glanced at the men around him and shook his head.

'We couldn't afford beer back on my farm,' he whispered, 'and . . .'

'Carter, if you just do what everyone else does, you'll be fine.'

'How do you get so wise?'

Lee rubbed his chin, then smiled. 'I'll explain in a way my pa once explained something to me.' Lee cleared his throat and placed a hand on his chest. 'Once, my friend, in a village at the foot of a great mountain, the corn harvest had gone badly.'

The conversation around him stopped and his fellow ranch hands leaned forward with their mouths open in anticipation of his tale.

Lee turned from Carter and waggled his eyebrows.

'And in this village,' he said, 'the village elder had two beautiful daughters.'

Everyone leaned closer.

After three mugs of beer at the trading post, Carter was glassy-eyed and Lee thought the room was spinning.

The other ranch hands had drunk three times as much as they had and were nowhere near as glassy-eyed. Neither was anyone discussing heading back to the Wayne ranch and beginning the day's work.

As Lee fingered his latest mug of beer, the horses whinnied outside.

As there were no windows in the trading post, Lee edged closer to Stem to ask him if he should investigate, but then the door flew open and three men slipped through the supplies and swaggered into the saloon area.

Moving jerkily, Stem and the other ranch hands turned to face the latest arrivals – Elliott Jameson, Orem Stack and Talbot Court. These men were smartly dressed, dust-free, clean-shaven, with lean builds and smirking superior smiles.

With hands on hips, they faced Stem. Then Elliott paced forward. He folded his arms and stared at Stem, from his sweaty brow to his scuffed boots, then back up to rest his gaze on Stem's wide paunch.

'Might have guessed you'd be stinking up this excuse for a saloon,' he muttered.

Stem ran the back of his hand over his mouth and breathed through his nostrils. Including Lee and Carter, Stem's group comprised ten men. The new group contained three men.

In an exaggerated lunge, Stem leaned forward and spat on the floor, creating a sticky patch in the sawdust between them.

'So, you're Alistair Marriott's new ranch boss. I hope you enjoy working for him,' Stem snorted. 'But then again, snakes enjoy each other's company.'

Elliott grinned and glanced along the row of ranch hands facing him.

'Lorne Wayne is a bigger snake than Alistair Marriott is, except he pays less and employs drunkards, no-hopers, and even Chinese. Things must get more desperate with every passing day.'

Lee slammed his mug on the table with a resounding crash.

'Lorne Wayne only employs the best,' he shouted, his voice louder than he intended it to be.

Elliott glanced at Lee and sneered.

'You're right, the drunkest drunkards, the most hopeless no-hopers and the smallest Chinese.' Elliott laughed and stared straight into Stem's eyes. 'Step aside, Stem. We're here for a drink.'

Stem squared off to Elliott. 'We don't drink with Marriott's ranch hands.'

'No problem.' Elliott shrugged. 'You can leave.'

Stem snorted again. 'We ain't moving.'

Elliott glanced back at the two men flanking him. They shared a chuckle.

Then, with a shouted oath, Elliott turned and charged at Stem with his head down. He wrapped his arms around Stem's chest and pushed him back against the table, which rocked, the barrels sloshing dangerously.

This was the only cue anyone needed, and within seconds Wayne's ranch hands had charged at Marriott's ranch hands.

From the back of the saloon area, Lee glanced at Carter, who also hadn't moved.

'A fair fight is one thing,' Carter said, 'but we outnumber them. Joining in just ain't fair.'

Lee nodded, but then one of Wayne's ranch hands, Dave, stumbled from the mêlée to land on his back, shaking his head. Then another ranch hand, Finch Calligan, landed beside him.

Wayne's ranch hands outnumbered Marriott's,

but the newcomers more than made up for their lack of manpower with their superior fighting skills.

Lee and Carter nodded to each other and leapt into the fray. Lee aimed his charge across the saloon area straight at Elliott, who had grabbed Stem's shoulders and was repeatedly slamming his back against the wall.

Lee slid to a halt. He grabbed Elliott from behind in a bear hug and tried to drag him to the floor.

Instead, Elliott kicked back, crashing his heel into Lee's shin. Pain shot up Lee's leg and he stumbled, catching his cheek on Elliott's flailing elbow. He collapsed.

Flat on the floor, Lee shook his head to clear it of the fog that threatened to fill his mind.

Elliott glared down at him. With a short kick, Elliott stamped at his fingers. Lee only just scraped them back before the boot ground into the floor. Then Elliott whirled round to slam Stem back against the wall again.

Lee jumped to his feet and dashed to help one of his fellow ranch hands, Mitchell, in his fight with Orem. He held his arms wide while he waited for an opening.

Mitchell and Orem shared two blows. Then Orem backed a step.

Taking this as his opening, Lee lowered his shoulder and at full tilt, he charged Orem. With a leading shoulder, he slammed into Orem's side and pushed him five paces across the room and straight into a barrel of beer.

They toppled over the barrel, landing in a heap on the other side.

With his senses muddled, Lee kept his head down and threw his arms up. He secured a tight grip of Orem's head and banged it against the barrel, then again and again.

As Lee hammered Orem's head for the fifth time, Orem reached up, slipped a stranglehold around Lee's neck, and pulled him down.

Lee thrust his elbow sideways. Soft flesh yielded as Orem gasped in his ear and rolled over the barrel.

With Orem prone, Lee leapt at him, but with surprising agility Orem rolled away and jumped to his feet, leaving Lee to slam into the floor.

Lee hunched away from an expected kick, but when the blow didn't come he looked up. At least three other men had bundled into Orem, and with a flurry of blows from all directions they pummelled him to the floor.

Lee rolled to his feet and dashed for the group, ready to join in the pummelling, but from behind, two wide arms wrapped around his chest.

With his feet set far apart, Lee flexed his elbow again, just as Stem shouted in his ear.

'Stop!' Stem roared. 'We won.'

Lee shrugged from Stem's grip to swirl around. Marriott's ranch hands lay flat on the sawdust-covered floor, but only five of Wayne's men were prone, Carter included.

As, one by one, the fallen fighters stirred, Lee shuffled across the saloon area to stand beside Carter.

Carter sat up and held his head.

'What happened?' he mumbled.

'We won,' Lee said. 'That's what happened.'

Carter touched his scalp and winced.

'Why does winning hurt so much?'

'Losing hurts more. Anything too painful?'

'Everything's too painful. Someone got a lucky drop on me.'

'Sure he did.' Lee laughed.

The bartender set a bucket of water beside them and Carter splashed a handful on his face, freeing a patch of his skin from the grime.

Lee glanced over his shoulder and smiled. Dave and Mitchell were passing another bucket of water to Marriott's ranch hands and checking that they were all right.

When everyone had availed themselves of a dunk in the water bucket, Elliott, Orem and Talbot rose to their feet. Elliott dragged them into a huddle. They shared low words, then broke up.

While rubbing his chin, Elliott glared at Wayne's ranch hands, who formed a line before the beer table. Elliott rolled his shoulders and spat on the sawdust-strewn floor.

'You beat us, but you outnumbered us by more than three to one,' he sneered. 'Think what would happen if we had even numbers.'

Stem laughed. 'Yeah, there'd be even more Marriott boys with sore heads.'

'You reckon?' Elliott bunched his fists.

'Yeah.' Stem swaggered across the saloon area and thrust his face to within inches of Elliott's. 'I reckon.'

The two ranch bosses stood toe to toe. Then Elliott smiled.

'Here's me reckoning I'm right and there's you reckoning you are.' Elliott rubbed his firm jaw. 'I guess there's only one way we can prove which one of us is.'

CHAPTER 7

'Flatten him!' Stem roared.

Carter faced Walter Faulk, his arms held out ready to grab his opponent the second he moved towards him. But Walter stayed back and started circling him with deliberate paces.

It was five hours after the impromptu fight in the trading post, and the hands from the Wayne and Marriott ranches had gathered at a shack on the border of both ranches' land.

They had marked out a circle in the centre of the shack, then formed groups on either side of the circle, each around a barrel of beer.

Then each ranch had selected eight men to fight one on one, after which the victors would eliminate each other in a process that would leave only one man standing victorious.

The only reward to the victor – the honour of working for the best ranch.

So far, the two fights had both gone to Marriott's ranch hands, but the luck of the draw had paired Carter with the shortest of the potential opponents.

Walter circled, his gaze never leaving Carter. Then Carter darted for him, aiming to wrap his arms around Walter's chest and bundle him to the ground, but Walter ducked under Carter's grasping hands and slammed his shoulder into Carter's guts.

Walter set his feet wide and lifted, meaning to hurl the larger man over his shoulders.

Carter's momentum almost carried him over Walter's back, but he jammed a foot in the ground and secured his footing. Then, instead of Walter throwing him over his shoulder, he crashed both arms around Walter's chest and held Walter bent double.

Carter rolled to the left, to the right, then bore down on Walter to knock him flat.

Walter tried to twist as he fell, but Carter had a firm grip and Walter's face slammed into the dirt, marking the end of this fight with victory to Carter.

Carter leapt to his feet and paraded in a circle around Walter. With the cheering from his side and the booing from the other side resounding in his ears, he pulled Walter to his feet and slapped him on the back, knocking him forward a pace towards his own men.

Then he sauntered back to his fellow ranch hands.

Stem slapped him on the back as he passed, then sauntered into the ring to face Orem, his opponent.

Carter swapped handshakes with each ranch hand before he joined Lee for further congratulations.

'You sorry not to be fighting?' Carter asked, still grinning wildly.

'Sort of,' Lee said. 'But even Walter's bigger than—'

A huge roar sounded around them.

They turned to see that Stem had flattened Orem within seconds of the bout starting, and now stood with a foot rested on Orem's back, his arms raised above his head.

Beneath him, Orem tried to squirm away from this indignity. But Stem didn't release his foot until the cheering on his side had started to wane.

Then he dragged Orem to his feet and with a mighty slap, pushed him to the Marriott side of the shack.

Stem swaggered back to his side, his fellow ranch hands cheering his every step. He joined Carter and shook his hand.

'We're getting a winning run now,' Carter said.

'Yup.' Stem slapped his belly. 'We'll show those Marriott boys which ranch is best.'

Carter leaned towards Stem. 'I got to ask. Aside from their obvious smugness, why do we hate Marriott's ranch hands so much.'

Stem sighed and glanced at the new fight starting between Dave and Talbot, then turned back to Carter.

'It wasn't always like this. Alistair Marriott and Lorne Wayne used to tolerate each other. We ranched this area in peace and built two of the finest ranches in the state. But ever since they found the silver load, they've done nothing but feud.'

Carter lowered his head a moment. 'It ain't my place to say this, but the Wayne ranch ain't that fine.

Back on our farm, we couldn't afford much, but it was a whole lot finer than Wayne's ranch.'

Stem glanced away, running a hand through his hair. He nodded and turned back to Carter, sighing.

'It used to be a fine ranch, but you're right, it ain't fine now. Soon as Lorne found silver, the thought of those shining nuggets drove away his interest in ranching.'

'But not Marriott?'

'Nope. He ranched and mined with equal vigour. That was bad enough, but a few months ago Lorne lost all interest in everything, and since then he's even stopped me maintaining the poor remnants of the ranch we have left. It's almost as if he wants it to collapse.' Stem shrugged. 'So all we got left now is to hate the Marriott boys.'

'And it's two fights all.' Carter nudged Stem in the ribs. 'I reckon that our luck is changing.'

Carter was wrong. For the next half-hour, his and Stem's victories were their only consolation, as win after win went to Marriott's ranch hands.

For the last of the first round of fights, the ranch boss, Elliott Jameson, strutted into the circle. He stood in the middle with his hands on his hips and a smirking grin plastered across his face.

Mitchell staggered into the circle to face him, but after the dinnertime drinking and further drinking in the shack, Mitchell was fighting a losing battle to stay upright.

In a shaking line, Mitchell wended towards Elliott and swayed to a halt. He set his feet wide and squared off to him, then, even though punching wasn't allowed and he was a good ten feet away from Elliott, he lunged a punch at him.

He succeeded only in throwing himself flat on his face.

Elliott roared with laughter, slapping his thighs and stamping his feet as his colleagues joined him and exaggerated their mirth.

'Fastest fight I've ever seen,' he shouted between laughs. 'It ended before it even started.'

Wayne's ranch hands hung their heads, muttering at this humiliation, but Lee leapt to his feet and with the blood pounding in his skull, he stormed into the circle. He stepped over Mitchell's snoring form and faced up to Elliott.

'If the fight was over before it began,' he shouted, 'I reckon there's still a fight to be had.'

'You do?' Elliott chuckled and glanced over his shoulder, hearing a wave of snorts and chuckling.

Lee spat on his hands. 'Yeah.'

Several of Marriott's ranch hands shouted their objection, but Elliott raised a hand, silencing them.

'I reckon if the little man wants some sense knocked into him, I can oblige.' Elliott licked his lips. 'With no punching, gouging or kicking, how does a man as small as you reckon he'll slam my face into the dirt?'

Lee glanced back at Stem, who winked his encouragement and with Carter, dragged Mitchell out of the circle.

Lee rolled his shoulders and took the longest pace he could manage towards Elliott.

'You're about to find out.'

Elliott shrugged. He retreated, beckoning Lee on, and Lee followed, keeping back from Elliott's superior grasping range, but looking for an opening.

Elliott backed another pace, but then his right foot slipped and, taking this as his chance, Lee charged him. Far quicker than Lee expected, Elliott righted himself and met Lee's charge with a strong forearm, which he blasted into Lee's cheek, knocking him on to his back.

Lee scrambled back, expecting Elliott to leap on him and finish the bout immediately, but his opponent just sauntered around him, shaking his head.

Lee jumped to his feet and dashed straight at Elliott, his head down and his arms waving in a berserk action that he hoped would confuse him, but Elliott just grabbed both Lee's arms and held up, then gripped both his wrists in one hand.

With his free hand, Elliott reached down, took hold of Lee's right knee, and hoisted the man aloft.

With cheering sounding from behind him, Elliott held Lee above his head and spun him round and round. Just as the dizziness forced a screech from Lee, Elliott threw him down.

Lee hit the ground and rolled, sliding to a halt in a cloud of dust. He shook his head, trying to free the sickness in his gut and the numbness in every limb.

He then levered himself up on a shaking arm.

He was facing his fellow ranch hands. They directed multiple shrugs and headshakes at him. In their midst, Stem looked down at him, also shaking his head.

'Stay down,' Stem mouthed.

Lee snorted and hurled himself to his feet. He stood a moment, swaying from the dizziness, then turned and charged at Elliott, flailing his arms as he fought for more speed.

Elliott stood his ground, his hands raised like a claw, ready to repel him. But at the last moment, Lee dived to the ground, slipping under Elliott's lunge for him and right through his legs. Even as he slid to a halt, he slammed both hands together and chopped them into the back of Elliott's right knee.

Elliott's leg flexed, knocking him to the side, and Lee encouraged the fall by grabbing his leg and hoisting him over. Elliott landed heavily on his side.

Lee leapt on Elliott and rolled him on to his front. Elliott shook his head and tried to buck Lee, but his effort was weak, and Lee thrust all his might into grinding Elliott's forehead into the dirt before he regained his strength.

Elliott's forehead closed to within a bare inch of the dirt. Lee strained to push him that last inch, but then Elliott slipped a hand from under his chest, and a gut-wrenching pain turned Lee's insides to water.

He fell from Elliott, unable to control his movements.

Elliott rolled to his knees, and with a mere flick of the wrist, rolled Lee over.

While whistling a merry tune, Elliott extended two fingers, placed them on the back of Lee's head, and dunked his forehead in the dirt. Elliott stood and bowed to his side, receiving riotous applause, then swaggered away from Lee.

Carter dashed to Lee's side and helped him sit up.

'What happened?' he said. 'You were winning.'

'Winning ain't that important,' Lee gasped, nursing his pain. 'After what Elliott just did to me, I'm wondering whether I can still have children.'

Carter winced. 'That's illegal.'

'Painful, too.' Lee held up a hand and let Carter drag him to his feet. Doubled over, he staggered back to his side. He glanced at Stem. 'Watch out for Elliott. He fights dirty.'

'No problem.' Stem shrugged. 'You just got to fight dirtier than he does.'

With only Carter and Stem winning in the first round of bouts, the six winning men from Marriott's ranch huddled up and decided who their best fighters were.

On the other side of the circle, Stem warmed up for his next fight by winning a beer-drinking bout with Finch.

Carter leaned to Lee. 'You were an idiot fighting Elliott when you didn't have to.'

'But I *did* have to.' Lee rubbed his guts, then drew Carter to the back wall of the shack. 'I knew Elliott when I was a miner. He was a supervisor, and he was the meanest of them all. Anybody that stood up to him was just looking to be thrown out of the mine with a beating for their trouble. I just wanted to repay him for all the misery he dished out.'

'Why is a mine supervisor now Marriott's ranch boss?'

Lee shrugged. 'Don't know. But—'

'Carter!' Stem roared.

Carter and Lee turned to see Brady Sanders striding into the circle, beckoning Carter to join him.

Carter rolled his shoulders and turned from Lee.

'Go on,' Lee said, patting Carter on the back. 'Get him.'

Carter slipped through the throng of backslapping ranch hands, then faced up to Brady in the circle.

The two men stared at each other a moment, then Carter charged at Brady, seeking to flatten him with his first move. He slammed into him, pushing Brady back a pace, but Brady planted his foot firmly back and, using it as a pivot, hurled Carter to the ground over his shoulder.

Carter rolled, avoiding having his face hit the dirt, but when he stopped his roll, Brady leapt on him and bundled him over on to his front.

With his feet planted on either side of Carter's shoulders, Brady sat on the small of Carter's back and grabbed his head in both hands. Inch by inch, he forced Carter's face towards the dirt.

Carter strained, his neck muscles bunching as he halted his downward path. Then, inch by inch, he pushed his head back up.

As the tussle reached a deadlock, Elliott sauntered across the circle to face up to Stem.

'Looks like it'll just be you to fight for the honour of your ranch,' he said.

'Carter will win this,' Stem said, nodding towards the circle.

With his face now a good foot from the ground, Carter flexed his back and tried to buck Brady away, but Brady just lifted slightly from Carter's back, the movement having failed.

Then, as Carter slumped down again, Brady hurled his feet up to crash down with all his weight on Carter's shoulders, slamming his face into the dirt.

Stem winced as Brady held his hands above his head, then stood. Brady waved in all directions, then leaned down and pulled Carter to his feet.

Lee dashed into the ring and helped Carter back to his side.

'Like I said,' Elliott muttered, sneering at Stem, 'it's just down to you and me.'

Stem rolled his shoulders. 'I'm looking forward to it. Ranch boss against ranch boss should sort out plenty of things.'

Elliott rubbed his chin. 'You want to make this the best of three?'

'Why?'

Elliott chuckled. 'Grinding your face into the dirt just the once won't satisfy me.'

'We stick to the same rules. Except, in the morning, you'll have a mighty sore head.'

'Marriott's boys ain't the only ones who'll have sore heads,' a voice boomed, echoing through the shack.

Elliott's mouth fell open and stayed open as he stared over Stem's shoulder.

Stem turned. His gaze rose until it reached the densely bearded face of the huge man who had set his tree-trunk thick legs astride in the doorway. Guns rested on both hips of this huge man, but his wide hands gripped the sides of the doorway.

'Abe Mountain,' Elliott whispered, 'is it you? Alistair said you were dead.'

Abe took two huge swaggering strides into the shack. He nodded, his wild beard rising and falling from his chest.

'Alistair probably said lots of things,' he boomed. 'Don't mean they're true.'

Stem paced from Elliott to look up at Abe.

'Lorne Wayne said the same. He said a landslide had trapped you in the mine.'

With his vast hands set wide on his hips, Abe glared down at Stem.

'You reckon they were right?'

As everyone in the shack shuffled backwards, Elliott strode forwards showing none of the fear that had permeated the shack. He stared up at Abe, looking like a child standing before an adult.

'I for one am glad to see you. Where have you been for the last three months?'

Abe ground his teeth, his beard swaying from side to side.

'I'd tired of the dust and the heat, so I headed south. But as it's just as dusty and hot down there, I'm back.'

Matching Abe's stance, Elliott slammed his hands on his hips.

'We go back a long way. If I'd have known you were alive, I wouldn't have given up working with you.'

Abe glared down at Elliott and flashed his shining white teeth.

'I believe you.'

Despite Elliott's seeming confidence, he breathed

a sigh of relief, then tipped his hat.

'What do you want me to do?'

With a wide finger, Abe pointed back through the shack door as he gazed across the rows of ranch hands.

'First up, come. . .' Abe's gaze settled on Waxman Franks, who was shuffling towards the door. 'You used to work for Alistair.'

Waxman shuffled another pace, then with a loud gulp, stared up at Abe.

'I worked for Alistair,' he said, 'but I had nothing to do with his deal with Marshal Brown.'

Abe shrugged. 'You had nothing to do with his deal, but you knew about a deal, which is more than I knew for sure ten seconds ago.'

In a blur Abe whirled his arms and grabbed a gun in each hand, the weapons puny in those great hams.

Waxman didn't reach for his weapon in the instant it took Abe to pull his two guns, so he just stared, agog.

Abe grinned. 'Are you going for your gun, or do I just kill you?'

Waxman gulped, then whirled his arm.

In an explosion of gunfire, Abe ripped two bullets straight through Waxman's chest. Waxman wheeled back to land face down.

Everyone else in the shack stood a moment then, in a shared moment of blind panic, they charged for the door. Those that couldn't reach the door dashed for the only window, and the others broke through rotted planks until they gained their freedom.

Lee was one of the first to slip outside, using his

small size to crawl through the legs of the group filling the doorway. He dashed away, then skidded to a halt and hurried back to help prise Carter outside. Then they dashed for their horses.

As the mayhem rippled around him, Abe just stood in the centre of the shack, his huge legs set wide, booming his laughter. Elliott stood at his side, chuckling.

The two groups of ranch hands finally found a route outside and they ran for their horses, mounted them with frantic haste, and galloped from the shack, heading for their respective ranches.

Lee glanced over his shoulder at the shack, which was now receding into the distance at a fast rate.

Abe and Elliott were sauntering outside to join another man who was waiting for them. They exchanged nods, then mounted their horses, but when they cantered down the trail, they headed towards the Marriott ranch.

Despite his confusion at what had just happened, Lee sighed with relief, then concentrated on riding as fast as he could.

CHAPTER 8

Alistair Marriott stood in the doorway to his imposing ranch house and glared at his ranch hand, Walter Faulk.

'You saw *what?*' Alistair shouted.

Walter ran his hands through his hair.

'It's Abe Mountain,' he babbled. 'He's riding here right now. Forget that Marshal Brown said he died in the mine. Abe ain't dead.'

Alistair closed his eyes for a moment. 'And where's Elliott?'

Walter raised his eyebrows. 'Varmint went over to Abe.'

'Then I got me a new ranch boss.' Alistair patted Walter's shoulder. 'Get everybody indoors.'

As Walter nodded and stormed away, barking orders, Alistair strode into his ranch house and collected his own gun.

It was four months since he and Lorne Wayne had ignored their feud about the ownership of the Silver Gulch mine and combined resources for one short and fatal month. That month ended with them asking Marshal Brown to remove the mine's troublesome protection man, Abe Mountain.

So Brown had lured Abe into a recently abandoned and unsafe mine tunnel and brought it down, supposedly killing Abe.

But Alistair prided himself on his scepticism and, despite the unsafe nature of the tunnel, he had crawled into it and, as he'd feared, aside from the rubble at the entrance, most of the tunnel was clear.

And, worst of all, he found no sign of Abe's body.

With a mixture of caution and desperation, Alistair surrounded himself with the best protection he could buy.

And then he waited for the worst.

When days, then weeks passed, he still expected Abe to return at any moment, but just as he was letting a nugget of hope rise in his heart that maybe Abe *was* dead after all, Walter had returned with this terrible news.

Alistair shook himself and stood tall, dragging his thoughts to the present.

For the next five minutes, the ranch hands hurried into the house, then Walter directed them to take positions by each window.

Alistair stood by a window and peered outside.

Three riders trotted through the gates. The central man was Abe Mountain. The others were Elliott Jameson and Rufus Tourney.

Elliott and Rufus had worked with Abe before Brown tried to remove him. Elliott worked in the mine. Abe worked on the outside. Rufus just caused trouble everywhere.

But after Abe's disappearance, against Alistair's better judgement he'd appointed Elliott as his ranch boss, figuring that someone as mean-spirited as Elliott would keep his new ranch hands in line.

As Alistair expected, Abe drew his tall horse to a halt out of easy gunfire-range of the house. He stood framed against the deep red sunset beyond. As Abe was such a big target, Alistair considered shooting at him, but if he wasted that chance, Abe would be devious enough to avoid giving him another.

Abe's booming voice rang out.

'Only two kinds of people are in there – those that are with me and those that are against me. The first type will live. The second type won't.'

'Brave talk,' Alistair shouted, pressed against the side of the window, 'except I have thirty men in here, and you have Elliott and Rufus. You're in no position to threaten us.'

'We only have fifteen,' Thomas, a lean ranch hand, whispered.

'When you open fire,' Alistair muttered, 'sound like thirty.'

Thomas wheeled round from his kneeling position beside a window and rested his rifle over an arm.

'Boss,' he said, 'perhaps I should sneak out the back and get the word out that Abe's returned.'

Alistair rubbed his forehead. Sweat drenched his skin, and not all of it caused by the oppressive heat. He nodded.

'Yeah, swing on out the back and get Marshal Brown to raise a posse.'

Thomas nodded, then ran to the back of the room

and through the back door.

'Elliott tells me that you only have fifteen men at most,' Abe shouted from outside. 'All hired mercenaries, paid the best rates. Except no rate compensates a man for being dead.'

'Stop talking tough and come in,' Alistair shouted through the window. 'Let's see how much longer you can cheat death.'

Abe threw back his great shaggy head and roared his laughter.

'I can cheat death for as long as I like. From where I'm standing, I can see you.'

Abe waved a hand over his head, and Elliott and Rufus cantered from him. Both men veered off diagonally to ride across the front of the house.

Then Abe ripped his two guns from their holsters, slammed the reins between his teeth, and spurred his horse to gallop at the house.

But within ten paces, he spat out the reins and pulled his horse to a halt. He raised a hand, halting the other two men, and glanced to his side.

Thomas trotted around the side of the house and scurried towards Abe, his rifle held high above his head.

'What is the fool doing?' Walter mumbled.

Alistair snorted. 'Thomas is double-crossing us – that's what the fool is doing.'

Thomas halted before Abe's horse, then lowered his rifle.

'Abe,' he shouted, 'I had no part in what they tried to do to you. If I'd known what was happening, I'd have stopped them. Now you're back, I'm with you.'

Abe glared down at Thomas, then nodded.

'Glad to hear it. As such, you live.' Abe turned from Thomas to glare at the house. He raised his voice. 'And if any other man joins me, they live, too. The rest die.'

Alistair glanced down the line of his carefully picked men.

Before Thomas had double-crossed him, Alistair had trusted his men. Now, he doubted them all.

But of the men in the house, only two had worked with him before Abe left. He backed into the centre of the room.

'Sullivan, Lanyon, step away from the window.'

'Why?' Sullivan said, turning on his knee to glare up at Alistair, his jaw set firm.

Lanyon matched Sullivan's belligerent stance.

'Because I want you where I can see you until we sort out this mess.'

With much muttering, Sullivan, then Lanyon, stood up. Sullivan moved forward deliberately to face Alistair.

'You're wrong,' he said. 'We're against Abe, too.'

Alistair snorted. 'Yeah, but step back, put your guns on the floor, and kick them over here. Then we'll all feel safer.'

Sullivan rocked back on his heels and glanced down the line of men at the windows.

The men glared back at him.

'Walter,' Alistair muttered. 'Take their weapons.'

Walter strode towards Sullivan with a hand out.

With a pained grin, Sullivan scratched his chest. Then he dragged his gun from its holster and spun on his heel to aim it at Walter.

'No one moves or I take them out,' he roared. 'I'm with Abe, too.'

'Yeah, me too,' Lanyon said, and scrambled for his gun.

Walter leapt at Lanyon, barging him to the floor with his shoulder.

Sullivan set his feet wide and sprayed an arc of bullets towards the men before the windows.

The men hammered repeated gunfire back into his chest.

As Sullivan staggered back to collapse over a table, Alistair dropped to his knees. Around him, gunfire exploded inside and outside the house.

CHAPTER 9

Stem organized his men into a tight group, with two riders staying back in case Abe doubled back and tried to ambush them.

But despite a few false alarms, when someone saw an animal or thought they heard a noise, each instance of which resulted in a sustained burst of gunfire in all directions, they reached the Wayne ranch safely.

Everyone quickly dismounted and dashed into the ranch house.

Flickering oil-lamps surrounded Lorne Wayne as he leaned against a log-filled fireplace and watched the ranch hands rush in. Years of ranching had weathered this thin white-haired man, and he had a coldness in his eyes that said something in him had died.

Stem approached Lorne and swung his hat from his head.

'Lorne,' he said, crumpling his hat, 'we saw Abe

Mountain back at the old shack.'

Lorne frowned, the barest flash of surprise flickering in his eyes. He gripped the wooden mantelpiece so tightly, all the colour drained from his hand. When he spoke, his voice was clipped and harsh.

'You'd better not be making a joke, or I'm looking for a new ranch boss.'

Stem wrung his hat, glancing around his men for encouragement.

'No, sir, I knew you'd say that, but we saw him and as you know, you can't mistake Abe.'

Lorne nodded and grabbed a poker. With long thrusts, he stabbed the fire, sending roaring swathes of flame into the chimney.

'You're right at that. Alistair shouldn't have trusted Marshal Brown. But it'd seem that Abe's mellower these days.' Lorne took a last lunge at the fire and threw the poker to the floor. 'You're alive to tell me that he's back.'

'Waxman wasn't so lucky. Abe took him out, no problem.'

Lorne fell back against the wall and tapped his fingers along his forehead.

'Did he say why he's returned?'

Stem slammed his hat on his head. 'Reckon we'll find out soon enough. But Alistair will find out first. Abe headed out to his ranch, and I don't reckon he went there for dinner.'

Lorne snorted a harsh chuckle. 'Except if he eats Alistair.'

Stem and several ranch hands chuckled with grim

humour, and for the first time, Lee spoke.

'Abe wouldn't do that, surely?' he asked.

With his gaze steady, Lorne turned to Lee. His eyes flickered with the hint of something, perhaps surprise, before he blinked it away.

'You're new around here, but you're right, Abe never ate anyone that I know of. But he'd do most of everything else.'

'So, who is Abe anyway?'

Lorne glanced around the group of men, all of whom either shivered or muttered to themselves.

'You should know what you'll face if you stay here. Abe arrived in Silver Creek after Alistair and I first found silver. He said he was a protection specialist and offered to guard any silver that we mined.' Lorne turned to the nearest window, his gaze beyond this place. 'But the protection was all from him. If we paid him the agreed cut, we had no trouble; if not, his men caused trouble.'

'So you removed him?'

'Not at first. Initially, Abe did keep trouble away, but he made bigger and bigger demands: five per cent of the profits, seven per cent, ten per cent. We paid him, but when he wanted twenty per cent, we had to do something. So, shortly after the. . .' Lorne gulped and glanced at Lee, then looked away. 'Shortly after the mining disaster, Brown. . .'

Stem shook his head. 'No use worrying about what did or didn't happen. We have us a situation, and I reckon we start by securing this house.'

A round of murmuring drifted around the room

and none of it was supportive. The ranch hands just glanced at each other with wide-eyed fear in their eyes and their shoulders bowed.

'But if he's attacking the Marriott ranch,' Lee shouted, 'practically single-handed, Marriott's ranch hands must stop him.'

Lorne smiled. 'They must, young man, and I hope they do, but you never take chances where Abe is concerned. We prepare for the worst.'

'And then we just sit here and hope that Alistair was successful, do we?'

'You're right. It'd help to know what's happening.' Lorne pointed over Lee's shoulder. 'And *you* need a lesson in what Abe is capable of doing.'

Lee winced. He turned to see where Lorne's finger pointed, confirming it aimed through the window, then turned back and drew to his full short height.

'What do you want me to do?'

'Head out to the Marriott ranch, then try to return alive to tell me what Abe is doing.'

Carter coughed and stood beside Lee.

'I'll go with him,' he said.

Lorne shrugged and waved a hand in dismissal, then returned to giving Stem instructions for the defence of the house.

Lee and Carter turned and shuffled outside. As they headed to their horses, Lee patted Carter's back.

'Thanks for coming,' he said, 'but you didn't need to volunteer, too.'

Carter laughed. 'Perhaps I reckon I did. Someone has to protect you from being reckless. For someone who's so wise, you don't know how to avoid volunteering for dangerous work.'

Lee winced. 'Reckon you're right.'

CHAPTER 10

On the floor of his ranch house, Alistair Marriott shuffled on hands and knees to Sullivan's side. He slapped a hand on his neck, confirmed that he was dead, then rolled to his feet and charged at Walter and Lanyon, who were rocking back and forth as they tried to throw each other to the floor.

He grabbed Walter's shoulder to drag him away and get a clear shot at Lanyon, but Walter shrugged his hand away and slugged Lanyon's jaw.

Behind him, a further explosion of gunfire blasted and this time it came from outside the house.

Ignoring the fight between Lanyon and Walter, Alistair swirled round.

A hail of bullets ripped through the windows. Three of his men plummeted to the floor, hurling their hands above their heads.

With glass exploding around him, Alistair crouched and steadied his aim towards the windows. Then the door flew back, ripped from its hinges to hurtle to the floor.

Everyone spun round to the doorway, but it remained empty.

A gunshot whistled over Alistair's head.

Lanyon had slugged Walter to the side. He crouched and aimed at Alistair.

Alistair dropped to the floor, lead blasting over his head, and shuffled his elbows into a firm position. He fired up at Lanyon. The first shot was wide and cannoned into the ceiling, but with his aim focused, he fired the second shot into Lanyon's left arm, a spray of blood blasting away.

As Lanyon staggered back, clutching his arm, he ripped another bullet into Lanyon's guts, then swirled round to face the door.

Thomas bounded through the broken window by the door, catching Talbot and Brady in his grasp as he fell to the floor.

Then Elliott leapt through the doorway, falling to his side as he spun round, firing and rolling at the same time.

Alistair tried to follow Elliott's rolling dive with his gun, but Elliott charged to the back of the room behind a table.

Alistair turned and ripped gunfire into Thomas's chest, but a bullet smashed Alistair's gun from his hand and gunfire exploded all around him. He turned towards the doorway.

Filling the doorway was Abe, a gun held in each hand as he fired continuously.

The ranch hands stood a moment, then most of them bolted for the windows. They leapt outside over the jagged glass shards and disappeared from view, nothing in their headlong dashes suggesting they'd ever return.

Only six men remained, and most of them scurried for cover behind the available tables and furniture.

With one gun discharged, Abe thrust the gun in his belt, grabbed a rectangular table in one hand, and swung it round to cover himself. With the table as a shield, he batted Brady through the window, then charged at the rest, bullets cannoning off the wood as he stormed across the room.

Alistair scurried to Lanyon's body. He kicked him over with the toe of his boot and scrambled for his gun. But as his hands brushed metal, Elliott leapt out from behind his covering table and grabbed Alistair around the neck.

'You ain't getting a gun,' Elliott muttered in Alistair's ear. 'We have plans for you.'

Thomas lay sprawled by the windows; he had been shot through the chest. Rufus knelt by his side, then shrugged and joined Elliott.

In the middle of the room, Abe stood with his legs set wide. He blasted Talbot aside with the table before he could get a clear shot at him.

Talbot hit the floor, rolled, staggered to his feet, and scampered for the window and outside.

But the four men who were left standing, Orem, Hank Wright, Pancho Max and Stanley Down, now kept out of his substantial range.

With no choice, Abe backed into a corner behind his table.

'Put your guns down,' Elliott shouted, thrusting

his gun against Alistair's temple, 'or I shoot your boss.'

Hank glanced at his gun, then lowered it a mite. But Pancho, Orem and Stanley glared back at Abe.

'Don't listen to him,' Alistair muttered. 'Elliott wants me alive or he'd have killed me. Take out Abe!'

Behind his table, Abe roared with laughter, rattling the surviving glass panes.

'You men weren't around when Brown tried to remove me, so I bear you no malice. If you join me, you can live.'

'Whoever kills Abe gets one thousand dollars,' Alistair shouted.

His men spread out across the room as Elliott dug the barrel into Alistair's temple.

'Alistair has made a nice offer,' Abe shouted. 'But whoever joins me gets an equal share in whatever I make out of this.'

Hank dropped his gun. Orem and Pancho lowered their guns. Only Stanley kept his gun pointed firmly at Abe.

Abe chuckled and threw the table to the side, where it landed ten feet away with an echoing thud. He folded his vast arms across his chest.

Stanley glanced at his gun, then whirled his hand to aim at Abe's head.

In an instant, Abe unfolded his arms and ripped a gun from its holster. He blasted two bullets through Stanley's chest before Stanley even tightened his trigger finger.

As Abe paced over Stanley's body to pat Pancho, Hank and Orem on their backs with a series of resounding thuds, Alistair struggled, but Elliott held him in a firm grip and turned him to face Abe.

With a huge stride, Abe halved the distance to Alistair. His beard waggled as he chuckled.

'Hiring mercenaries was a mistake. Guns hired by the dollar turn against you as soon as someone makes them a better offer.'

Alistair gulped and backed to press against Elliott, but Elliott pushed him forward.

'What do you want from me?' Alistair said, trying to keep the fear from his speech, but still hearing his voice shake.

Abe loomed over Alistair and grinned, revealing two endless rows of gleaming white teeth.

'I have a new contract for the mining rights to the Silver Gulch mine.'

Abe reached into his buffalo-hide jacket, pulled out a folded sheet of paper, and hurled it at him.

The paper bounced off Alistair's chest, but Elliott released his grip and nudged him forward.

Alistair grabbed the paper. With as much confidence as he could muster, he strode to his writing-desk by the back wall, unfolded the sheet and read the contents.

The document he unfolded was a copy of the contract he'd signed with Lorne Wayne and Marshal Brown four months ago, but with an additional clause and three signatures at the bottom. As his own signature was there, they were clearly forged.

Alistair turned to Abe and raised his eyebrows, his confusion not outweighing the fear that had seized his guts and wouldn't let go.

'What do you want me to do with this?'

'I want a copy.'

'If you insist,' Alistair murmured.

He removed a pen and sheet of paper from his desk. He flattened the paper and secured it with a glass paperweight, then reached for a pot of ink.

With a great clawing hand, Abe dashed the pot away and it smashed against the wall.

'You ain't filling the pen with ink. You're copying the contract in blood, your blood. And you'll draw it yourself.' Abe chuckled and slammed his fist on the writing-desk. The paperweight fell and smashed on the floor. 'You have a letter-opening knife. It's blunt, but it should do.'

Alistair glanced at the knife on the writing-desk, then tore his gaze away.

'I ain't doing that.'

With a huge fist, Abe slammed the writing-desk, which creaked and splintered. He loomed over Alistair, thrusting his huge head to within inches of Alistair's cringing face.

'You will, or your suffering really starts.'

'All right,' Alistair whispered.

He kept his mind blank and grabbed the knife.

With a last glance up at Abe's piercing blue gaze, he pressed the knife against his forearm. Then, breathing deeply, he tried to move his hand downward, but the hand shook with an involuntary tremor.

From above him, Abe chuckled, the sound grating in Alistair's mind.

'Make sure you draw enough blood. I want a

perfect copy. If I find any mistakes, you'll write it out again.'

Alistair winced and sliced the knife down his forearm.

CHAPTER 11

Lee and Carter rode down the darkening trail from the trading post to the Marriott ranch.

They were just below the brow of a hill, when from ahead, gunshots blasted and echoed. They glanced at each other, then rode in silence over the hill.

The Marriott ranch appeared ahead. The ranch house windows were open. Harsh light from within burned down on the sparse scrub.

Lee led as they cantered down the trail to the ranch gates. In the light from the house, their horses would be visible to anyone in the house, but from here they could make a quick escape.

Keeping as close to each outhouse as possible, they edged towards the house in a semicircle. They stayed in the shadows as they shuffled past a stable, a barn and two derelict buildings to reach the side of the house.

Lee leaned around the corner of the house. Several windows were broken, with one destroyed, the frame lying in shredded lengths of timber on the porch.

Conversation drifted from the windows. The voices were low and determined. Then a scream ripped through the muttering, echoing in Lee's mind and chilling his blood.

He started, stumbling back against the wall. Carter jumped, too.

To return his heartbeat to a normal rhythm, Lee took deep breaths, but then another scream pierced the night. It sounded animal.

Lee had heard people in pain before, fallen timbers having crushed them, but these screams were stronger than he'd heard before.

'Stay here,' Lee whispered, and patted Carter's shoulder.

He took a last deep breath and knelt. With deliberate care to avoid the shards of broken glass, he crawled around the side of the house and on to the porch to lie beneath the first window. He listened to the conversation inside. From the volume of one of the voices, he guessed it was Abe.

'I can't read this word,' Abe roared. 'This ain't good enough. Write the next copy correctly or this *will* be a long night.'

Lee lifted his head and looked through the broken window.

Bullet-ridden bodies hammered at his attention and blotted out everything else. He counted three spread over a table, a chair and by the window.

With a supreme effort, he tore his gaze from the bodies. In a chair thrust behind a desk, one man sat, hunched and facing the back wall. Elliott loomed over him, gripping his shoulders.

Spread around them, five other men leaned around the desk and the back wall, grinning; most were men who had been fighting in the shack just a few short hours ago.

With his back to Lee and partly hiding the man at the desk, Abe slammed his hands on his hips and grunted an order.

Another scream pierced the night.

Lee ducked. For five heartbeats he lay on the porch. He heard no more, so he lifted his head to look over the windowsill.

Inside, Abe had moved aside and the man at the desk had turned from the back wall. The man held a knife. Slowly, he drew the knife across his own bared chest. Blood welled around the wound and dribbled over the man's hand.

Lee gulped and crawled from the window to join Carter.

'What's happening?' Carter asked.

Lee glanced back at the window where brightness streamed into the night, creating an elongated rectangle of harsh light on the ground.

'Some of Marriott's ranch hands are dead. I guess the rest have run. One man is left. I think he's Alistair Marriott and. . .' Lee gulped. 'Abe's torturing him.'

'Do we help him?' Carter's eyes were wide, the surrounding grime on his face helping to brighten them in the faint light.

Lee shook his head. 'No. We have to report to Lorne.'

Carter ran an arm over his forehead, wiping away a sheen of glistening sweat, and glanced at the house, then back to Lee. When he spoke, his voice was low and deliberate.

'I'll look before we return, so I can report, too.'

Lee shook his head, but doubled over, Carter shuffled past Lee and along the porch to the first broken window. He lifted his face over the windowsill and peered inside.

Carter flinched, then stood beside the window.

To plan the quickest route back to their horses, Lee turned and examined the outbuildings. But a clatter sounded and he swirled round.

Carter had leapt on to the windowsill and stood in the window with his gun thrust forward.

'Everyone put their hands up,' he shouted, 'and stand back from Alistair.'

Lee's heart thudded. Then, seeing no choice but to join Carter, he dashed along the porch and leapt on to the windowsill of the second broken window.

'Like Carter said,' Lee shouted, 'every man to the back wall. Move real slow or there'll be trouble.'

Abe turned from the red-stained desk, grinning, and stroked his long beard. From his elevated stance on the windowsill, Lee shared Abe's eye-line.

'I recognize you from the shack,' Abe said, lowering his voice. 'If Lorne is employing more people like you, taking him will be even more fun than I expected. Now run along and tell Lorne I'm coming to get him as soon as I've finished with Alistair.'

Lee snorted. 'We ain't running along without Alistair.'

'You sure are feeling brave tonight. As you asked nicely, you can take Alistair. But you'll have to wait until I've finished with him.' Abe chuckled. 'If what's left can move, you can take him.'

Lee glanced around the room, judging his chances. Like Abe, the men facing him had their arms crossed, except for Elliott, who was holding down Alistair. Only Alistair appeared interested in their presence, his eyes red-rimmed and staring.

With a short gesture, Carter waved his gun towards Abe.

'Step away from Alistair. This is your last warning.'

Abe roared his laughter, the sound louder than Alistair's screaming. The oil-lamps rattled as Abe threw his head back, his beard bouncing on his chest.

By degrees Abe's laughter faded away and he looked back down. Hs smoothed his beard, still chuckling.

Abe crouched and a shot exploded from a gun that seemed to appear in his hand from nowhere.

Carter cried out and a thud sounded as he fell on to the porch.

Lee aimed his gun towards Abe, but before he could fire, Abe had swirled to him, his vast body turned on the hip. Abe crouched, one hand with the palm facing down above his gun hand.

'What's it to be, little man,' Abe said, grinning, 'are you feeling brave?'

Lee's stomach turned to ice. In a sudden decision, he leapt backward as lead whistled by his head. He landed on his back with a crunch. He rolled to his side and pushed himself to his feet.

'Hank, get them,' Abe shouted from inside.

Lee crawled quickly along the porch to Carter's side

'You all right?' he murmured.

Carter nodded. 'He nicked my arm, but I don't think it's serious.'

Lee glanced at Carter's arm. A dark patch was spreading from beneath the usual grime. He patted Carter's shoulder, then pointed to the ranch gates.

Carter nodded. They rolled to their haunches and kept their heads down as they scurried away. When they cleared the blocks of light on the ground, they stood tall and dashed across the open ground towards the gates.

Lee glanced over his shoulder, but nobody was following them and Abe was still in the house.

'They ain't following,' Lee shouted. 'Let's hope this is our lucky day.'

'Nope,' a new voice said from beside them. 'Your luck just ran out.'

Lee skidded to a halt and swirled round as Hank strode forward a pace, his form silhouetted against the night sky, his gun reflecting light from the house.

'How did you get there so fast?' Lee snapped.

'More to the point,' Hank said, 'why were you so slow? But you're coming with me. Once Abe has enjoyed himself with Alistair, he'll want dessert.'

A wave of pure panic grabbed Lee. In desperation, he leapt to the side. He hit the ground with his shoulder and turned the dive into a roll towards the gates.

A burst of gunfire blasted into the ground behind him, pebbles hammering his heels. He rolled to his feet, slid in a cloud of dust, and bolted, head held low.

Someone shouted. Lee glanced over his shoulder. Carter hadn't run with him, but had leapt at Hank, wrapping his hands around Hank's midriff and bundling him to the ground.

Lee skidded to a halt and dashed back to the struggling twosome.

Hank threw Carter from him and his opponent landed a yard away on his back. Kneeling on the ground, Hank aimed his gun at Carter.

A gunshot ripped through the night. Hank fell down to face the stars. Dust billowed around his body. Dust-eddies drifted in stray beams of light from the house windows.

Lee gulped. With his hand shaking, he slotted the gun back into its holster and tottered five paces to stand over Hank.

Carter jumped to his feet and dashed to him. He grabbed Lee's elbow and pointed to the gates.

'I shot a man,' Lee whispered, his breath ragged.

'Yeah, I know.' Carter dragged him a pace towards the gates. 'And you'll have to shoot a whole lot more men if we don't get out of here now.'

Lee let Carter turn him from Hank. Then, as his legs regained their feeling, Lee broke into a run and dashed to his horse.

At the gates, Carter helped Lee into the saddle, then he unhooked their reins from the gate and leapt on to his own horse.

Lee glared back at the house, his heart hammering inside his skull. Within seconds, the numbness that had hit him when he'd killed Hank faded from his limbs, and in its place hot blood pounded into his veins. His heart thudded, the sound filling his mind.

'Get 'em,' he roared.

He flicked his horse's reins to the right and spurred the animal on. Recklessly, it bolted straight for the house.

'Lee,' Carter shouted behind him. 'Don't!'

But Lee was galloping for the house.

When his horse charged into the light before the house, Lee pulled back on the reins. The horse came to a skidding, prancing halt. Through the window, he saw Abe's gang milling around Alistair at the back of the room.

Lee dragged out his gun. He blasted three shots at the men, but his horse bucked beneath him and the shots cannoned into the wall above the windows.

Inside, Abe swirled round, glaring at him through a window.,

From Abe's twin guns, an explosion of light ripped out, and with a terrible, almost human, scream, Lee's horse buckled to its knees, then tottered over.

Lee leapt clear of his dying horse to land on the ground flat on his stomach, the impact blasting the breath from his body.

On the ground and groggy, Lee pushed to his knees. Then, around him, further gunfire blasted. Most came from the house, but some wild shots came from Carter, who was galloping towards him.

Carter dragged his horse to a skidding halt and thrust a hand down.

Lee glanced inside the house, but as the men

inside hurtled to the windows, their guns out and ready, Lee angrily slapped his fist against his thigh and let Carter pull him on to the back of his horse.

He slotted in behind Carter, who, with one last wild shot over his shoulder, urged the horse to a gallop. They leapt over Hank's prone body and through the gates, bullets peppering the fence posts beside them.

Then they were deep into the night.

With his brief flurry of anger fading from his mind, Lee glanced back.

In the receding blocks of light before the Marriott ranch, the only man he could see was the prone Hank, and nobody was pursuing them. But a tortured scream ripped from the house and echoed in the night.

Still they galloped on.

When they reached the first hill, a faint scream drifted to them, distant and difficult to differentiate from the usual night-time animal noises.

But with gritted teeth, Lee hung his head and let Carter ride down the darkened trail.

CHAPTER 12

As soon as they cantered through the gates into the Wayne ranch, Lee and Carter dismounted.

Carter led his horse into the stable, while Lee leaned on the stable door, trying to calm his breathing, and stared at the crescent moon as it emerged from behind low cloud.

But the hollow numbness had returned.

When Carter wandered from the stable, Lee grabbed his arm.

'Thank you,' he said. 'You saved my life.'

Carter shrugged and tipped back his hat.

'I lost track of who saved who. I nearly got us killed when I tried to rescue Alistair. I attacked Hank, but you shot him. Then you tried to rescue Alistair, and I had to help you.' Carter hung his head and kicked the stable door. 'Either way, I'm not proud of what we did. We left Alistair to die.'

Lee hung his head as well. Taking up the rear, he let Carter wander into the house first.

Inside, Lorne glared at them, then glanced at Stem.

'Stem, get these boys a drink,' he said. 'No need to ask them what they've seen at the Marriott ranch.'

'Obliged,' Lee and Carter murmured together.

As Stem rummaged in a cupboard by the wall, clattering bottles inside, Lorne leaned forward.

'Not that I don't want to know what you saw.'

Carter removed his hat and batted it against his leg, freeing a flurry of dust.

'In brief, most of Marriott's ranch hands ran. Those that didn't are either dead or have gone over to Abe.'

Lorne turned and spat in the fire, producing a short sizzling explosion.

'Can't say that running or turning on Alistair isn't typical of the men he hired.' Lorne sighed and lowered his voice. 'What about Alistair?'

'Dead,' Carter said, his voice catching. 'Although . . .'

Lee coughed. 'When we left, Alistair was still alive, but we reckon that he was wishing he was dead, and he'll get that wish soon.'

Lorne nodded and turned to stare into the fire, his eyes blank, the faintest of smiles curling his mouth.

Stem handed large whiskies to Lee and Carter. Lee, then Carter, knocked back a gulp.

Stem stalked across the room and leaned on the wall, facing Lorne.

'Unless you got a plan in mind,' he said, 'it'd seem that we don't stand a chance.'

Lorne glanced at each of the ten men inside the

room, obviously assessing which ones would run, which ones would stay, and which ones would turn against him.

At least three of the men were wide-eyed as they glanced repeatedly at the door.

Lorne coughed and pushed himself from the wall. He set his feet wide and folded his arms.

'Men, Alistair paid good wages to attract a certain type of man. I've done my best by you and I've always paid a fair rate, but at times like these, you deserve more. So, I'm doubling everyone's wages for a month if they stay and face Abe.'

Dave, a haggard ranch hand with a permanent downtrodden expression, kicked a chair, pushing it back across the floor.

'Double pay ain't any good to a dead man.'

William Ellsworth grabbed Dave's shoulder and spun him round to face him.

'Nobody but Abe has to die if we stick together. The way I'm seeing it, this Abe can't be as tough as everyone says he is.'

This comment received a round of snorting and a chuckle from Lorne.

'That's as maybe,' Dave said, with his head bowed. 'On his own, we might stop him, but he has some of Marriott's ranch hands, too. We have no hope.'

Lorne slapped a fist against his thigh until the murmuring agreement died down. Then he faced his men.

'We do have hope. None of Marriott's ranch hands are as dangerous as Abe. Remove Abe and the rest will fall apart. That was Alistair's plan three months ago and it nearly worked. Got no reason to suppose the plan won't work this time.'

Although some men nodded, Dave shook his head.

'Except Abe has the likes of Elliott Jameson. Maybe he ain't as mean as Abe is, but he's bad enough.'

Lee strode three paces to stand before Dave. He slammed his hands on his hips.

'Elliott is bad, but Hank ain't so tough any more.' Lee knocked back the rest of his whiskey and hurled the glass at the wall. 'Because I killed him. And that's one less man for you to worry about.'

Dave opened his mouth as if he was about to argue, but then lowered his head and shuffled back to the wall.

Finch snorted and took Dave's place.

'I was never worried about the likes of Hank,' he said. 'Abe is the main threat. He's the meanest shot I've seen.'

As everyone hung their heads again, Lee stormed into the centre of the room. He padded round in a circle, staring at each man in turn, shaking his head.

'You're making out that Abe is some kind of indestructible man. He ain't. He's fallible. From just feet away, Abe shot at me and missed.'

'Don't believe that,' Finch said, shaking his head.

With a flat hand, Lee mimed a bullet whistling over his head.

'Not by much.'

Carter joined Lee in the centre of the room and patted his arm.

'Me, too. Abe ain't as good as you think he is. He only winged me.' Carter drew his sleeve round and pointed at the ragged hole. 'And I'm ready and eager for the next round.'

Brooding silence and bowed heads greeted this comment, until Finch snorted.

'Sounds to me like you're making this up.'

'You saying we is lying?' Carter swirled round and squared off to Finch, arms extended, his large hands clenched into fists.

As Finch bunched a fist, Lorne stepped between them and raised his hands.

'We ain't fighting each other,' he muttered, then glared at Finch. 'I don't reckon Carter and Lee are lying, but I don't reckon they understood the situation, either. I presume if Abe nicked Carter's arm, that's what he was aiming for, and if he missed Lee, he must have had his reasons.'

Carter frowned. 'I don't reckon so.'

'Either way, we can't spend all night arguing.' Lorne mirrored Lee's steady padding round in a circle as he glared at each man in turn, his gaze cold. 'I'm not persuading you to do something that you don't want to do. Whoever has the guts to stay, stay. The rest can leave.'

Dave, Finch and William glanced at the door.

'Mr Wayne,' Lee shouted, 'from what we overheard at the Marriott ranch Abe believes Alistair double-crossed him. How did he do it?'

'It's a long story and there ain't time.' Lorne glared at Dave, who stood stooped, staring at the door from the corner of his eye.

Lee strode across the room to stand beside Lorne. He placed a hand on his shoulder.

'Sir, in this situation we might appreciate hearing how someone nearly beat Abe before.' Lee gripped his hand more tightly. 'I'm sure that tale would give us hope.'

Lorne sighed. He lowered his head a moment, then looked up, a hint of wetness in his eyes as he looked at Lee.

'I'm surprised that you want to hear about that again. You worked down the mine. I'd have thought you'd have learned more about Abe than most people have.'

'Before today,' Lee murmured, 'I'd never seen or heard of Abe.'

With his eyebrows raised, Lorne backed a pace.

'I'm surprised. Abe spent a lot of time at the mine, ensuring it operated smoothly.'

Lee sneered. 'I was underground. I didn't get many opportunities to enjoy the scenery.'

Lorne turned from Lee's firm gaze and nodded.

'Perhaps not, but you must have been around during the mining disaster four months ago.'

'I can hardly forget it,' Lee snapped. 'I lost family and friends when that tunnel collapsed.'

Lorne turned his gaze back to Lee, his eyes bright.

'Abe demanded an increased share of the mine. Alistair and me were arguing – just like we always did – about how we resolved the pay dispute, but we agreed to refuse him. So, Abe brought a tunnel down. Didn't matter to him that twenty-seven miners were working in it. Afterwards, I had to let Alistair join forces with Marshal Brown and remove him. It's a tragedy that when Brown brought down the tunnel on Abe, he didn't kill him.'

Lee slammed his fist against his thigh and stormed to the nearest window. There, he dropped to his knees and glared into the darkness outside.

'I'll stay,' Finch said.

'Do what you want,' Dave said. 'I'm not ready to die.'

Lee gritted his teeth, blocking out the argument from his mind.

For long moments his mind stayed in a fugue until he noticed Carter's reflection in the window, sitting beside him. Still, he kept his gaze through the window.

'Lee,' Carter said, his voice low but resolute, 'whatever the others do, I'm staying.'

'No need. I have to stay. I can't walk away knowing what Abe did, but you don't have to stay. This is my battle.'

'If it's your battle, it's mine, too.'

'Thanks.' Lee glanced at Carter and forced a short chuckle. 'But you should go. I can take care of myself, but you can't fire a gun properly. You'll get yourself killed.'

Carter pushed away from the window and returned, clutching a rifle.

'You're right. I don't have much skill with a gun, but I'm a mean shot with this here rifle.'

'A rifle *is* a gun.'

'Sort of, but back on my farm, we couldn't afford guns. But we could afford rifles for shooting birds and rabbits.' Carter grinned. 'And men don't move as fast as birds do.'

Lee laughed, enjoying feeling the tension in his guts diminish.

'Yeah, I reckon you're right at that.'

They settled on either side of the window and peered into the darkness, waiting for Abe to come.

Along the length of the windows, the other defenders also stared into the night.

It was only when another hour had passed that Lee noticed nobody had left.

CHAPTER 13

The morning chill wrapped around Lee as he stared through the window.

Carter tapped his shoulder and held out a steaming tin cup of dark, pungent coffee. The warming smell drifted into his nostrils.

Lee nodded his thanks. For the first time since the previous evening, he holstered his gun, then rubbed his raw eyes.

With a creaking flex of his fingers, he took the mug from Carter and huddled over the coffee, letting the warmth seep into his tired bones.

Degree by degree his spirits livened as he gulped down the brew, but just as he reached the dregs, Lee saw movement outside.

Against the horizon, cresting the nearest ridge, a lone rider emerged.

Lee nudged Carter, who nodded and whistled.

As the ranch hands knelt by their windows, five

more men trotted into view and stretched across the ridge.

The man in the middle was Abe. Even when sitting he was a head taller than the rest.

At a steady trot, the riders slipped through the ranch gates and drew to a halt ten yards in from the gates. Abe trotted forward a horse-length.

'I only bear a grudge against one man inside,' he shouted. 'So, the rest can choose whether they want to live or die. You have one minute.'

Lee leaned close to the window and steadied his gun arm.

Each of the ranch hands stared through their own windows, their jaws set firm, their guns held out, a self-respect in their steady gaze which Lee hadn't seen before.

Abe spun his horse round and murmured to Elliott.

Elliott grinned. Then, with a whoop of bravado, he dragged his horse to the right and led the riders in a line before the ranch. They arced round and disappeared from view around the side of the house.

Inside, everyone glanced at each other and shrugged, but as there was only one way into the building, and that was from the front, they returned to staring through the windows.

The riders completed a circle of the house, but Elliott led them across to the front again. They disappeared from view around the corner of the house, only to reappear a minute later at the other side of it.

On this circuit, the riders drew back, creating a wider gap between themselves and the rider in front, and they increased their speed.

Lee closed his eyes a moment to avoid staring at the mesmerizing blur of horses charging before him.

Then he realized something.

Five men had started circling, but on this pass he'd only seen four men.

'Boss,' he shouted, 'one of the riders hasn't followed them round.'

As the riders slipped around the corner, Lorne pointed at the furthest windows on either side of the room and ordered Dave and William to guard against the attackers gaining positions on the sides of the house.

As Dave and William dashed to the flanking windows, a crunch sounded from above, and then a hammering.

Everyone glanced at the roof, but then Elliott led his horses on another pass.

On this pass, Abe fired a single shot, which clattered into the wall beside Lee's window.

Outside, each rider then fired when he was at his nearest point to the building. Each shot clattered above the widows or plumed into the dirt in front of the house.

But the men inside judged that they were just trying to rile them and didn't return fire, preferring instead to let them waste bullets. The riders disappeared from view around the corner again, but this time their trail of hoof prints was inside the line they'd created previously.

On their next pass before the house, the first three riders each fired a single bullet. Again each shot was wild, although Elliott smashed a bullet through the window above Lee.

Glass cascaded round him, but Lee avoided ducking and as soon as Elliott was level with the window, Lee let rip with a speculative shot through the broken window.

The riders returned a volley of gunfire.

All around Lee, the windows exploded. He ducked and so did the other defenders.

Lee bobbed up above the windowsill and fired back, but the riders were already galloping around the side of the house.

The man on the roof hammered again.

Lee rubbed his chin, then leapt to his feet and faced Lorne.

'Sir,' he shouted, 'no man could break through the roof, could he?'

Lorne concentrated his gaze on his window and firmed his gun hand.

'Nobody could.'

'But Abe might.'

'He's in the line of riders outside.'

Lee shook his head. 'That last volley could have been a distraction.'

Lorne, then everyone else, looked up as with a crashing and grinding of timbers, a wide block of the roof collapsed.

In a blast of dust and timber, Abe hurtled to the floor through the ruined roof. He landed on bent knees, a fence post held aloft. With a vast fist, he clubbed Lorne aside then swirled round to face the other men.

Lee dashed towards Abe, but the eight-foot fence post blurred towards him. Abe was wielding it with just one hand. Desperately, Lee leapt to the floor and the post whistled over him, clipping his shoulder as he fell.

Without stopping, the post hurtled round in an arc, scything Carter and the next three men in seconds.

On the ground, Lee rubbed his shoulder, then staggered to his feet and tottered towards Abe, pulling his gun as he fought to regain his senses.

To avoid the swirling post, Stem and William dropped to the floor. But even as the few men whom Abe hadn't scythed down were dragging themselves to their feet, Orem and Pancho crashed through the windows to face the ragged survivors.

Lee turned on his heel and ripped a shot into Pancho's guts.

Pancho went down, clutching his chest, but Orem barged into Lee, forcing his gun arm upwards. An involuntary trigger-pull wasted a shot into the ceiling.

Orem ripped the gun from Lee's hand and the two men rocked back and forth, but then with a wry smile to himself, Lee swung his leg up, slamming his knee between his opponent's legs. Orem folded, and Lee pushed him away to face Abe.

Abe was swinging the fence post on a second arc, scything through Stem and William. Then, with everyone but Lee pole-axed, he rocked the post back on a shoulder and glared down at him. He chuckled.

Lee glanced around, confirming that all the defenders were down. Orem was climbing to his feet, and outside, Elliott and Rufus were galloping towards the house.

'What's it to be, little man?' Abe roared.

Lee stood tall. 'You'll take Lorne over my dead body.'

Abe nodded, his vast beard rising and falling. He smiled with an arc of gleaming teeth.

'If you insist.' Abe swung the fence post high above his head, but as Lee stared up at him with his chin jutting, he hurled the post against the wall. 'Your threat just forced me to retreat.'

Abe swaggered past the open-mouthed Lee to Orem. He hoisted Orem to his feet and marched outside, the climb through the broken window barely breaking his stride.

'But we have them!' Orem shouted, but already they were outside.

Lee staggered to the window, his thoughts more confused then they'd ever been in his life.

He peered outside to watch Abe collecting Elliott and Rufus. The two men yelled their disagreement at Abe and gestured back at the house, but Abe silenced them with one harsh glare, and without further argument, the four men retreated to hide behind an overturned cart before the barn. There, they hunkered down out of view.

Carter staggered to his feet and joined Lee at the

window, rubbing his chest.

'Why did he do that?' he asked, his voice high and bewildered.

Lee shrugged. 'No idea.'

'He must have recognized you. But why did you scare him off?'

'Like I said.' Lee tipped back his hat. 'I got as much idea as to why he didn't kill me as you have.'

Lee rubbed his eyes, trying to shake off his confusion, but when that failed he turned and helped Carter get the other men to their feet.

As each man stood, they asked the same question as Carter had, but only Lorne ventured an answer.

'I reckon Abe is just making us suffer,' he said, rubbing his head.

For the fifth time in as many minutes, Lee shrugged. Still bewildered, he joined everyone in resuming their positions by the broken windows.

When long minutes had passed, and Abe and his gang still stayed behind their cart, the ranch hands accepted that death wasn't imminent and counted through their injuries. None were severe and they had lost no men.

Abe had lost the one man whom Lee had shot – Pancho.

For another ten minutes they waited, but Abe still remained behind the cart, nobody even getting a sight of him or any of his men.

'Maybe they've run away,' Finch said.

Such was the bemusement that everyone still felt, a general murmuring agreement drifted around the room.

'Perhaps Finch is right,' Lorne said. He looked around at his men, rubbing his chin, then strode to Lee's side. He glanced at Lee, then at Carter. 'You two did well reporting back from the Marriott ranch. You up to another mission?'

CHAPTER 14

Lee and Carter galloped back into Silver Creek.

Thirty minutes earlier, they'd sneaked out of the ranch while Stem and the others had blasted off an impressive amount of covering gunfire.

Abe's gang, if they were still hiding behind the cart, returned no shots.

Then they'd dashed to the stable and galloped away on Lorne's fastest horses. Nobody had pursued them.

In Silver Creek, the town was its usual raucous self, even in the morning. Music blasted from the saloon and people bustled around as they filled the roads with excited chatter.

They wended a path through the thronging people outside the saloon and headed to the end of the road and the marshal's office. They tethered their horses and dashed inside.

Marshal Brown glanced up from his desk and winced.

'I had a feeling you two would be back. The job of

deputy town marshal is still open, and as soon as an applicant who ain't Chinese and who ain't an idiot walks through that door, I'll hire him. Until then, you two are just littering up the place.'

Lee shook his head and set his squat legs wide.

'We ain't here about the deputy's job. We got desperate news.'

Brown yawned. 'I'll listen, and if it ain't a wild story, I'll pay.'

As Carter muttered inaudibly under his breath, Lee ground his teeth, forcing himself to keep his anger bottled.

'Abe Mountain is back.'

Brown snorted. 'You two *are* desperate. That's the third time today some idiot has tried to sell me that ridiculous lie. I didn't pay the first two, and I ain't paying you.'

'We didn't ask for money,' Carter hissed.

'Then you're even more stupid than I thought.' Brown pointed to the door. 'Now get out here before I arrest you for vagrancy.'

Lee stormed across the office, slammed both hands on Brown's desk, and glared down at him.

'We're here for your help. Abe has killed Alistair Marriott and all of his ranch hands who got in the way. He's holed up at the Wayne ranch now, aiming to kill Lorne. We need you to round up a posse and get out there.'

Brown sneered. 'And I don't believe a word of that.'

Lee spun around from the marshal, mumbling, but Carter joined him and set his hands on his hips.

'Marshal,' Carter said, 'who told you that they'd seen Abe?'

'Roger Vickers from the trading post. Then some ranch hand who works for Alistair, Brady Sanders.'

'And would you normally trust those people?'

'Nope.' Brown pointed a firm finger at the door. 'Now get out before I throw you out.'

'You can do that.' Lee smiled. 'But once Abe's killed Lorne, he'll come for you. He knows you tried to remove him, and he ain't impressed.'

Brown's eyes widened. He gulped.

'How do you know that I removed Abe?'

'Abe told us.'

'It can't be,' Brown murmured, his eyes now frantic and glancing all around his office. 'Abe is dead.'

'He's alive, and he'll come looking for you, unless you round up that posse real fast.'

Brown glared at Lee, then at Carter. He nodded curtly, then jumped to his feet and stormed past them to the door, grabbing a gunbelt as he went.

Carter coughed. 'We'll come with you.'

Brown shook his head and turned back.

'No. You two stay here.' A devious smile spread across his face. 'I need my deputies to look after my office when I'm not here.'

Despite the situation, Lee grinned.

'You mean you're hiring us?'

Brown walked to the door and stood with his back to them. He nodded.

'Yup, I've reconsidered.'

'You're too late,' Carter snapped. 'We ain't interested. We work for Lorne Wayne now.'

Brown leaned on the doorframe and glanced over his shoulder.

'Whatever Lorne is paying you, I'll double it.'

Carter glanced at Lee, who returned a nod.

Lee smiled. 'Looks like you got two new deputies.'

Brown snorted, then strode outside, slamming the door shut behind him.

Carter whistled through his teeth. 'Yesterday, we were on half-pay. This morning, we were on full pay. Now, we're on double pay. I reckon life is sure looking up.'

'Yeah.' Lee sat on Brown's desk. 'But only if we live long enough to enjoy it.'

For the next ten minutes, Lee munched a hunk of hard bread, while Carter stared through the window down the main road.

Then Carter coughed and beckoned Lee to the door.

From down the road a horse was heading for Brown's office, and Rufus Tourney was riding it.

Lee pressed his face to the glass and searched for more members of Abe's gang, but he saw only Rufus.

Ten yards from the door, Rufus dismounted and faced the office. He shuffled his feet into the ground.

'Marshal Brown,' he shouted, 'come out. We have unfinished business.'

Lee glanced at Carter, who shrugged. Lee cleared his throat.

'He ain't interested in your business.'

Rufus laughed. 'That sounds like Yick Lee inside. You get around.'

'I'm *Deputy* Yick Lee now.'

Rufus shrugged. 'Don't matter to me none. My quarrel is with Marshal Brown. Send him out now. But if you defend that coward, I'll kill you.'

'What d'you reckon?' Lee whispered to Carter.

Carter patted his rifle. 'I reckon I've had enough of hiding, and that Rufus is annoying me.'

Lee nodded and threw the door open. He paced on to the porch. With Carter beside him, he faced Rufus.

Lee shuffled his shoulders in his jacket.

'We deputies have a duty to uphold the law. As you're threatening a lawman, we're arresting you.'

Rufus glared at Lee, then at Carter, and laughed.

'Yesterday, you were another dropout working for Lorne. Now, you're a deputy.' Rufus snorted. 'Now, quit jesting and tell Brown to come out.'

'If you want him, you'll have to go through us.'

'I hoped you'd say that,' Rufus muttered. His grin widened.

Rufus rocked his right shoulder down. His hand whirled to his holster.

Lee dropped to the ground, a bullet hurtling by his head. By his side, Carter blasted a slug at Rufus, but Rufus hurled himself to the side, Carter's shot winging past his shoulder.

Lee ripped out his gun and rolled to his side. On his belly, he slammed both elbows on the ground and, as Rufus rolled to his haunches, he blasted him through the chest.

Rufus toppled back. He twitched once, then was still.

With his smouldering rifle dangling from his

hand, Carter glanced down the road. Despite the gunfire, nobody had ventured closer to the office.

'Where is Marshal Brown,' Carter muttered, 'and where is that posse?'

Lee jumped to his feet and joined Carter in the road. He rubbed his chin, then nodded.

'Unless he hasn't stayed in town to raise a posse . . .'

'But where would he go?'

'I reckon if you think for a moment, there's only one place he'd go.'

Carter glanced down at the body of Rufus in the road. He nodded.

CHAPTER 15

Lee and Carter galloped out of Silver Creek, their jaws set firm. Despite having been recently deputized, neither man fancied their chances of raising a posse, so they had no choice but to find Marshal Brown first.

They'd agreed that Marshal Brown's scepticism in Abe's resurrection would force him to seek proof that Abe's body was at the mine.

And worse, the arrival of Rufus suggested that Abe had wanted him to take Brown there to face him.

The sun was high in the sky, beating down with relentless heat as they rode along the dusty trail to the trading post.

Instead of taking the route to the Wayne ranch, they veered towards the mine and headed into the winding pass that ultimately led to Silver Gulch.

From a mile away, they received the first sign that they were approaching the mine, as the noise grew.

A clamouring of metal hammering against metal, and metal hammering against ground as hard as metal, filled the hot dry morning. Underpinning the industrial sound was the babble of workers giving orders, arguing, or discussing, but the conversations merged into a solid wave of sound.

Once they'd turned the last corner in the approach to the mine, the sight was as hideous as Lee remembered from when he'd first arrived two years before.

The mine was a vast gash in the side of what was once probably an elegantly rounded hill, now a quarter demolished as the surface prospectors converted it into large rubble, then smaller rubble, then dust. All day long, these desperate men searched for the seams of silver and occasional pockets of gold.

And, like an iceberg, this industry was just the tip of the horrors here.

Carter stared at the mine with the same open-mouthed expression that Lee had, when he first saw this mixture of the worst place on Earth and the most wondrous. Too much happened for the eye to understand and, not knowing what to look at, newcomers always darted their vision back and forth, trying to take everything in at once.

Sadly, Lee knew that before long you'd discover the mine lacked any wonder. All you found was grime, pain, sweat and more grime. Riches existed, but you'd see those only in other people's hands.

'What are all the people doing?' Carter shouted.

Enough men dashed about to mean that you could never work out what they all did, but Lee pointed to the top of the gash in the hill.

'At the top, they chip or blast the rocks. Then they roll the pieces to the bottom. There, they grind it down and wash the spoil to find silver. But those men don't work officially for the mine. They're scavenging, hoping to find nuggets in the spoil that the real miners have discarded. If they find something, they eat. If they don't, life gets tough.'

Sadly, many of these people only scurried from boulder to boulder, searching rocks that other people had already searched a hundred times, deluded in their belief that they possessed an observational skill nobody else had.

But that was just a small part of the mining operation.

Carter waved his arm in a wide arc, signifying the dirty, over-populated hill.

'Which part of this did you work on?'

Lee also waved his arm in a swathe across the hill.

'Do you see any Chinese people here?'

Carter shook his head. 'I can't tell. These people could have bright green skin and you wouldn't know. Everyone's so filthy.'

'Well, they ain't here. What you can see is only a fraction of the mine – the nice part. I worked underground. Beneath our feet are miles of tunnels and hundreds of men, hammering at the walls, all day, every day. If you want to know what real filth is, you need to go down there.'

Carter kneaded his brow, his lip curled in disgust.

Lee dismounted and strode towards a man wearing a peaked cap, who stood outside a tent. The cap signified his status as a supervisor, an essential requirement since he was encrusted in the blanket of grime that everyone gained within hours of arriving here.

Lee talked to him, using gestures as much as words to counteract the noise that was concentrated into an almost physical force at the foot of the hill.

'Where is Marshal Brown?'

The supervisor turned to Lee. 'Who wants to know?'

'Did Marshal Brown come here? We need to find him. His life is in danger.'

The supervisor smirked. 'Being a marshal in a town like Silver Creek, his life is always in danger.'

Carter dismounted and joined Lee.

'We have to find him,' he yelled.

The supervisor snorted and glared at Lee. 'You and your grinning friend can stop wasting my time, and return down the mine. We have schedules to meet.'

'I ain't from the mine,' Lee muttered. 'I'm Marshal Brown's deputy.'

'Yeah, sure, and I'm Marshal Brown's horse. Now, return to work or you're fired.' The supervisor turned from Lee and headed back to his tent.

With a clawed hand, Lee reached out to grab the supervisor and shake an answer from him, but Carter grabbed his arm and pulled him back a pace. He cupped his mouth over Lee's ear.

'We're wasting our time,' Carter said. 'The supervisor knows everything that goes on here, and nobody has told him they've seen Abe.'

'How can you know that?'

'If someone saw Abe, they couldn't fail to recognize him and they'd tell the supervisor. As he's calm, that ain't happened.'

Lee glanced around the hill. Above him, hundreds of dirt-encrusted workers milled around the dozen or so mine entrances.

'Where do you reckon we search, then?'

Carter also gazed over the hill.

'The way I see it, if Brown tried to bury Abe in a tunnel, that's where they'll be. Which tunnels were closed four months ago?'

Lee pointed down the pass. 'They're on the other side of the pass.'

They mounted their horses and backed a hundred yards down the pass, then picked a route up the side of it, over a rocky ridge, down into another pass, and around the base of the hill on the other side.

Away from the main mining activity, several smaller entrances were dotted about the hills, but they were all half-blocked in and clearly had not been used for some time.

Lee put his hand to his brow and peered around the surrounding hills. When his gaze reached a rocky crag, he saw movement.

Lee pointed and, with Carter, edged up the side of the crag.

When they'd ascended around fifty yards, Lee saw further movement and as they swung around to climb the steepest part of the crag, a horse's tail, then a horse, came into view. He couldn't see a rider, but as he crested the main crag, he confirmed that the horse was tethered to a boulder, and from the size, it was unmistakably Abe's horse.

Better still, Marshal Brown's mount stood ten feet away from this horse.

With these two animals filling most of the outcrop, they dismounted thirty yards back. Lee trapped his horse's reins beneath a rock. Carter matched his action, and they scrambled up the rocks to the mine entrance.

The entrance wasn't as blocked as the other entrances were, but from the spindly vegetation clogging the rocks, it hadn't been used for a while.

They edged past a pile of boulders and shuffled into the darkness beyond. Lee was about to ask Carter if he had anything with which they could produce light, but then he noticed a faint glow ahead.

The tunnel veered to the left, and at the corner, light and shadows reflected along the tunnel wall. Although they were faint, from fifty yards Lee saw that the shadows were of people.

They stalked down the tunnel, Lee leading, placing their feet on the pebble-strewn ground as quietly as possible.

Half-way to the corner, low voices reached them. Another ten yards on, Lee recognized Brown's voice.

'This'll do you no good,' Brown said, his voice clipped and on edge. 'But just get this over with. Do your worst.'

A chuckle sounded, and from the deep tone, it clearly came from Abe.

'You don't want to know what the worst I can do is.'

In the sudden silence, Lee edged to the tunnel corner. With his face pressed as close to the wall as possible, he peered around the corner.

Brown was backing against the wall of the closed-in tunnel. Facing him stood Abe, his outline edged in light from a flickering oil-lamp, his vast shadow cutting back across the tunnel.

With a wide hand, Abe reached into his jacket and pulled out a sheet of paper.

'This is a copy of the contract that worm of a lawyer in Bear Rock created when you received my share of the mine.'

Abe hurled the contract at Brown.

Brown caught and glanced at it.

'I ain't signing this.'

'No problem.' Abe ran a hand over his shock of hair, the hand brushing against the tunnel roof. 'I've already signed it for you, and as you'll be dead, you won't be able to tell anyone that it ain't your signature.'

'I didn't want to own any part of this dirt-filled hill.' Brown threw the contract back at Abe and folded his arms. 'I was just glad to rid the town of trash like you.'

Abe pocketed the contract and chuckled.

'You're not pleading for your life like Alistair Marriott did. You still got the chance.'

'I ain't, because I don't reckon you want me to trap you a second time.' Brown glanced at the tunnel roof and grinned. 'I chose this tunnel carefully last time. It's the least stable one around. And now, it's even less stable. One gunshot and the rest of the tunnel will collapse.'

Abe ran his hand over the tunnel roof, as if he might hold it up. He broke off a stalactite and threw it to the ground, then glared at Brown, his hands on his hips.

'You wouldn't bring down the tunnel on yourself.'

'Better the death I choose than the one you've planned for me. Either you back off, or I kill us both.'

'You don't have a death wish,' Abe said.

Carter edged back and looked over his shoulder, judging the distance to the entrance, then shared a glance with Lee, but Lee drew his gun and stepped around the corner of the tunnel.

'Marshal Brown might not have a death wish,' he said, 'but I have.'

Abe swirled round. With his huge legs set wide, he filled the tunnel.

'You again,' he muttered.

With his gun, Lee gestured to the roof.

'I have no qualms about bringing down this tunnel. You killed twenty-seven miners, and you ain't walking from here alive.'

Chuckling, Abe paced a large stride towards Lee. Flurries of dust rained down from the roof to coat his hair and beard. 'It takes more than rocks to kill me. Marshal Brown couldn't do it. Neither can you.'

Lee backed to the wall and gritted his teeth.

'Brown doesn't understand mines, but I've spent too long down here.' Lee gripped his gun more tightly and aimed it at the roof above Abe's head. 'I know how cave-ins start. And when I bring this tunnel down, nobody will walk out of here alive.'

Abe roared with laughter. He threw his head back

and laughed long and hard. Large flurries of dust cascaded around him. When he stopped laughing, he smiled down at Lee.

'Don't die down here, Yick Lee.' His voice was softer than Lee had ever heard before. 'Only this scum of a lawman deserves that fate.'

Lee snorted and firmed his gun hand.

'No more talk. Step aside and let Brown leave.'

Brown edged to the side, aiming for the gap in the tunnel beside Abe.

'You're going nowhere,' Abe roared.

'And neither are you.' Brown grabbed his gun. 'We have you where we want you.'

With a whirl of his arm, Abe ripped his gun from its holster, the weapon coming to his hand in an instant. His single shot sliced into Brown's chest, blasting him back against the tunnel wall.

A deep rumbling sounded in the tunnel.

Brown staggered a pace from the wall, clutching his chest. He removed the shaking hand and glanced at his reddened palm. Then, with a grim smile, he ripped two bullets into the tunnel roof.

A boulder plummeted from the roof to crash down beside him.

Lee glanced up, seeing another boulder shake loose, and in desperation he dashed to the side and dragged Carter from the tunnel wall, an explosion of dust and rocks cascading around him.

They bolted down the tunnel with their hands over their heads, gritting their teeth against the stones bouncing off their shoulders and arms.

Abe shouted, the words unrecognizable, but they

receded into the distance as a deep rumbling filled the tunnel.

Pace by desperate pace they closed on the tunnel entrance, but Lee slid to a halt, turned and fired another two bullet into the roof.

These final gunshots doubled the rumbling from further down the tunnel. Timber beams creaked and exploded around them, and vast plumes of dust and debris peppered their backs as they ran.

With a final burst of speed, they bolted and leapt from the tunnel entrance, throwing up their arms as they landed in a rolling pile outside. At their heels, huge gouts of dust and stones hurtled from the tunnel as the entrance collapsed.

On the ground, Lee sat and stared at the funnel of dust rippling into the air from the tunnel entrance, which within seconds closed to a tangle of debris. He batted dust from his clothes, a grim smile on his lips.

Carter stood, the dust providing a lighter layer of grime to his clothes, and watched the clouds of dust coming from the tunnel entrance, then turned to Lee.

'Were you serious about bringing down the tunnel?'

Lee sighed. 'Guess we'll never know now.'

Carter patted Lee's shoulder and headed from the rock-filled entrance.

'In that case, we'd better get back to the Wayne ranch and finish—' Carter flinched as another vast belch of dust funnelled out of the remaining small gap.

'Don't worry. There'll be plenty of rumbling until

the earth settles to a new level.'

With a hand to his brow, Lee stood on the edge of the outcrop and picked the safest route down the crag to their horses.

'You're another one who ain't sneaky enough,' a voice roared. 'You won't kill me when I can see death coming.'

Lee swirled round.

Abe stood in the tunnel entrance, pushing boulders aside. With dust coating his huge body, he looked like a ghost.

But this ghost was alive.

CHAPTER 16

Lee glared up at Abe, who stood framed in the ruined tunnel entrance.

Abe chuckled and slammed his huge hands on his hips.

With a lunge, Lee drew his gun. Beside him, Carter scrambled for his rifle.

Abe dropped his hands to his sides.

Twin blasts of gunfire sounded. A bullet tore Lee's gun from his grip. A simultaneous blast winged Carter's rifle to the ground.

With his guns held high, Abe stalked from the tunnel entrance to stand before Carter and Lee.

'Stop toying with us,' Carter muttered.

Abe slipped his guns back into their holsters and shook his head.

'I have no desire to kill another miner.'

Carter shrugged, and with his head down, he charged at Abe. He ran to within two yards of him, but, with a lunge of a large hand, Abe batted him away as if he were a fly.

Carter landed on his back ten feet away. He shook

his head and stared up at Abe.

With the loudest roar he could manage, Lee dashed to Abe and with his fist bunched tight, thumped him in the stomach. He felt like he had hit iron. His hand numbed as he staggered back.

Abe smiled. 'Run along, Yick Lee. You have much to live for.'

Lee kicked Abe's shin, but he only deadened his own foot.

Carter jumped to his feet and charged at Abe. With his fists gripped together over his head, he slammed them against Abe's chest.

Abe chuckled. 'You need to be sneakier than that to kill me.'

Abe flicked up a hand and smashed Carter beneath the chin.

Carter's head cracked back. He hurtled against the rock face and slumped to the ground, his head lolling to his chest.

With a backhanded swipe, Abe knocked Lee the other way.

Lee hit the ground and skidded ten feet, but when he stopped he shuffled round to glare up at Abe.

Abe advanced a long pace, and in desperation Lee rolled away, but he landed on a hard object. With a sudden flurry of hope, Lee pressed his chest down and confirmed that the hard object was his gun.

Keeping his movements hidden beneath him, Lee pushed the gun under his jacket and staggered to his feet, holding his stomach as if he were hurt.

Abe smiled and reached into his jacket. With two thick fingers, he extracted the contract and threw it towards Lee for it to land five feet before him in a cloud of dust.

Lee ignored the contract, but kept his gaze on Abe, looking for an opportunity to pull his gun.

'Read the contract,' Abe roared.

Lee glanced at the contract on the stony ground.

'Don't need to. I saw what you did to Alistair to make him sign away his rights.'

Abe threw his head back, chuckling, and when his head came back down to stare at Lee, the grin that split his dirt-streaked face gleamed brilliant white in the sunlight.

'Yeah, Alistair sure hollered when I made him write that contract a third time.'

Lee winced and wrapped a finger around the trigger beneath his jacket.

Abe's chuckling grew into a vast peel of laughter and again he threw his head back, his face turned to the sky, roaring his delight.

Taking this as the chance he was waiting for, Lee pulled the gun from his jacket, but unable to kill Abe in cold blood, he waited until Abe's laughing meandered to an end.

Abe's great head lowered. He narrowed his eyes.

'You have a gun. You're sneaky, perhaps sneaky enough.' Abe licked his lips. 'But you should have killed me when I wasn't looking – that's the only way you'll do it.'

Lee held his gun at arm's length. From five yards, he couldn't miss Abe. The man nearly filled his vision. He steadied his arm and kept his gaze on Abe's hands, waiting for the tell-tale twitch that'd indicate that Abe was about to draw.

'Perhaps, but I give people a chance, even a murderer like you. You'll see proper justice. It's what my brother and friends deserve after you buried them somewhere in that hill.'

Abe glanced back at the tunnel entrance, where dust still plumed out, and nodded.

'I guessed as much. If it helps, I'm sorry.'

Lee pointed the gun more firmly at Abe.

'You won't distract me. Twenty-seven people died in that mine. Sorry ain't good enough.'

'You're right.' Abe lifted his hands high from his guns, none of his former good humour remaining. 'But I didn't kill those miners.'

'Am I supposed to believe the word of a murderer like you?' Lee depressed his trigger finger a mite.

Abe shrugged. 'The only people I tried to kill, tried to kill me first. If you want to blame anyone for those miners' deaths, blame Alistair and Lorne. I may have pulled the beams out and brought the tunnel down, but I didn't know any miners were in there. Alistair and Lorne *did* know. They're the murderers.'

Lee blinked hard, then swiped away a layer of sudden sweat from his brow.

'Why would they do that?'

'To end the pay dispute.'

Lee snorted. 'How can I believe you?'

With a low chuckle, Abe shrugged. 'You can't. But read the contract and you won't need to believe me.'

From the corner of his eye, Lee glanced at the contract on the ground. Without moving his gaze from Abe, he dropped to one knee and grabbed the document.

With one hand, he batted open the folded paper and held it up to read it. Most of the contract contained convoluted legal words, but at the bottom was a final clause in large handwriting above three signatures.

Lee glanced up, his mouth wide open.

'This is a trick.'

Abe batted the dust from his beard.

'No trick. I returned to Silver Creek to right wrongs.'

For the first time, Lee let his gun drift from Abe, and stabbed the gun barrel against the contract.

'If Lorne Wayne ain't alive to contest this, you could have sole ownership of the mine, but you're handing over your rights to the miners.'

Abe nodded. 'Every last one of them. There'll be plenty of fairly wealthy people tonight. That's better than having two rich people.'

Lee shook his head. 'You killed twenty-seven miners. You can't buy your way out of that.'

Abe set his jaw firm and folded his arms.

'I didn't know that I was killing those miners, and I'm not trying to buy my way out of anything. I'm just righting a wrong in my own way.'

Lee staggered back a pace, kneading his brow with his free hand.

'And as I'm a miner, you didn't kill me when you had the chance.'

Abe nodded. 'Yeah. I promised myself I wouldn't kill another miner when I removed the vermin that have ruined Silver Gulch.'

'Lorne Wayne lied to me.' Lee lowered his gun, then lowered his head a moment. 'And I won't shoot you.'

'I know. You ain't sneaky enough, either.'

Abe tipped his hat and sauntered to Lee. He loomed over him and bent to rip the contract from his hand, then strode to his horse.

'Where are you going?' Lee shouted after him.

Abe mounted his horse, then looked back down at Lee.

'Removing Lorne.' Abe pointed a firm finger at Lee. 'Don't do anything foolish. Stay away from the Wayne ranch until this is over.'

Lee opened his mouth to demand more details about the events at the mine which had so ruled his life for the last four months, but then shook his head in bemusement.

Abe pulled his horse to the side and wended a path down the steep side of the crag.

With his hands on his hips, Lee watched Abe until he was just a vast blob of colour at the bottom of the crag. Then he wandered to Carter's side. He slapped Carter's cheek, receiving a few groggy mutterings, then pulled Carter to his feet.

'Did you hear any of that?' Lee asked.

'I heard some.' Carter prodded the back of his head, wincing. 'Did you believe him?'

'He didn't kill me. And that's the sort of proof I like.'

'But I'm no miner, and he could have easily killed me.'

Lee glanced at Carter's grimed clothing.

'I reckon he thought you were so dirty, you had to be a miner, too.'

Carter smiled. 'Perhaps you're right. But will that contract be valid? I've never heard of miners sharing ownership of a mine.'

'Don't see why not.'

'So, what will you do with your share? You'll be rich soon.'

Lee shook his head. 'Nope. The contract splits the rights to the mine amongst the miners, but I ain't a miner any more. And I never will be again, whatever the incentive.'

'What are you now?'

Lee smiled. 'I'm Silver Creek's deputy town marshal – just like you.'

Carter set his hands on his hips. 'So, as deputies, what are we doing about Abe riding off to kill Lorne Wayne?'

Lee glanced down the side of the crag at Abe's receding form.

'I reckon I'll follow Abe and see that justice is done.'

Carter paced round to stand before Lee.

'And what will be justice?'

'Lorne dying, of course.'

'You're siding with Abe!'

'I didn't say that. But Lorne Wayne helped to organize the mine massacre, and if Abe aims to kill him, that's all right by me.'

'And what about all the other people at the ranch? If anyone stands before Abe, he'll kill them to get at

Lorne. And Stem and the others are decent men.'

Lee sneered and moved to walk past Carter.

'If they protect a murderer like Lorne, they're just as bad as Lorne is and deserve what they get.'

Carter grabbed Lee's shoulder and spun him back.

'You're wrong. They're working men, like you and me. They ain't got a choice.' Carter stared deep into Lee's eyes, his gaze firm. 'And if you let Abe kill them, you're the one who's just as bad as Lorne is.'

Lee stared back at Carter, then lowered his head. He kicked a stone, then nodded and tipped back his hat.

'Seems you make a better lawman than I do.' He faced up to Carter. 'What do you reckon we should do?'

Carter blew out his cheeks and scratched his chin.

'I reckon you were right about one thing. We have to see justice done here. We've heard Lorne's version of the feuding over the Silver Gulch mine. Then Abe told you a different story. Neither you nor I know which story is true. So, we have to keep Abe and Lorne apart and let someone else sort out the truth later.'

Lee nodded. 'All right. You try to round up that posse. I'll get back to the ranch.'

Carter turned to his horse, then turned back.

'And who is that posse aiming to arrest?'

Lee shrugged. 'We'll just see about that when they get there.'

CHAPTER 17

Carter galloped into Silver Creek and swung round to pass the marshal's office.

The body of Rufus had gone, so he galloped to the Hot Silver Saloon, where he dismounted, tethered his horse, and charged inside.

In a barrage of orders and oaths, he pushed the saloon folk aside until he cleared a path to the bar.

At the bar, he grabbed a glass. He slammed it on the bar, slammed it down again, then maintained a continuous rhythm of slamming it down.

When all conversation in the saloon died, he slid the glass down the bar and faced the room with his hands on his hips.

'I'm rounding up a posse,' he shouted.

'Why in tarnation is a ranch hand rounding up a posse?' Silas Malt called out.

'Because I'm *Deputy* Carter Lyle now. Marshal Brown has been killed, but just before he died he deputized me. So, as I'm the nearest thing Silver Creek has to a lawman, I'm looking to round up some men to bring his killer to justice.'

Silas stepped forward, then another man, and with a wave of nodding and shrugging, several other men joined the group.

'Any idea who killed him?' Silas asked.

'It was Abe Mountain.'

A pronounced series of gulps sounded.

'It can't be. Abe Mountain is dead.'

'You ain't the first man to make that mistake. But with your help he'll be in custody by sundown.'

Silas snorted. 'We ain't heading out with you to chase ghosts.'

Carter glared at Silas, but from behind Silas, Brady Sanders pushed back from the bar.

Brady wended through several other men who, until yesterday, were also Alistair Marriott's ranch hands, but were now trying to drink the saloon dry.

'Carter is right,' he said, his speech slurred. He barged into the clear space before Carter and waved his whiskey glass in the air. 'Abe is back, and he ain't in a good mood.'

Brady staggered round to face the line of potential posse volunteers. He mimed firing in all directions, sloshing his whiskey about him.

With plenty of sideways glances, Silas edged back into the crowd of saloon folk and, one by one, his fellow volunteers edged back to melt into the crowd, too.

'You can't do that,' Carter roared. 'We have to get Abe!'

'We don't have to face Abe,' Brady said. He tottered round to face Carter and knocked back the remains of his whiskey. 'Not when we enjoy living so much.'

'You ain't letting one man scare you, are you?'

'Yup, when that one man is Abe Mountain.' Brady rolled to the bar and banged his empty whiskey glass on it. 'I reckon staying here and supping whiskey is the best place any man can be when Abe is around. And I suggest you do the same.'

'I ain't. I'm walking out of here now to get him.'

'Then I hope you got plenty of luck.' Brady laughed. 'Or a fast horse, to get away as fast as possible when he turns on you.'

'I don't need luck or a fast horse; I just need a posse.' Carter raised his voice so that it echoed through the saloon. 'And any man that doesn't come with me is a coward.'

Brady glanced along the row of Marriott ranch hands, receiving a wave of snorts, then he slumped over the bar.

Carter set his hands on his hips and glared around the saloon.

He failed to meet anybody else's eyes, but he still turned and strode to the batwings as slowly as possible.

In the doorway, he hung on to the doors a moment, then pushed through to stand on the boardwalk with his arms folded.

For long moments he stood, balancing up and down on his heels as he waited, hoping that someone would follow him out.

From inside he heard subdued conversation, but nobody emerged.

With a snort, he turned to look into the saloon.

Inside, Brady and the other drinkers were ordering more whiskey.

'You're all cowards!' Carter bellowed.

The drinkers hunched over the bar, studiously avoiding looking through the door at him.

Carter slammed his fist against his thigh, then stormed off the boardwalk. He mounted his horse and swung it round. He patted a fistful of bunched reins into his other hand four times.

Then, with a last glance at the Hot Silver Saloon, he galloped out of town, heading for the Wayne ranch.

CHAPTER 18

Lee galloped across the dusty plains, a huge funnel of dust rippling behind him. As Abe had headed back on the main trail, Lee had no choice but to head across country to reach the Wayne ranch first.

By his calculation, Elliott and Orem were the only members of Abe's gang that were still alive and, sure enough, when he reached the ranch gates, only two men were hunkered down behind the cart before the barn.

Elliott swung his gun towards Lee, but a holler sounded from the house and a sustained blast of covering gunfire ripped around the cart. Elliott and Orem dived for cover, giving Lee the chance to hurtle to the house, dismount, and dash inside.

Once inside, Lee quickly told everyone about Marshal Brown's fate and Carter's attempt to round up a posse. He reduced the encounter with Abe to just the fact that Abe was heading here.

While he relayed this information, he searched Lorne's eyes for any hint of the duplicity he now reckoned Lorne had committed, but Lorne's gaze was firm as he listened to Lee's tale.

When Lee had finished, Lorne just ordered everyone to hunker down beside the windows and await Abe's return.

Ten minutes later, Carter was the first to arrive.

Stem ordered his men to cover him, enabling Carter to scurry into the house safely.

'How did you get past Abe?' Lorne shouted, as Carter slammed the door shut behind him.

'I headed across country,' Carter said, removing his hat to wipe the sweat from his brow. 'But Abe's only a few minutes away.'

'And where's that posse?'

Carter hurled his hat to the floor. 'The posse ain't coming. The good-for-nothing men from the Marriott ranch are just as scared of facing Abe as they ever were, and the rest of the townsfolk are even more worthless.'

Lorne nodded. He strode to the window and stared outside. Framed against the sky on the closest ridge was Abe Mountain.

'Then it's just us against him. If we're resolute, we can fight him off like we did the last time. We outnumber him, and even Abe can't beat the odds every time.' Lorne glanced around his men. 'You all ready?'

Stem slapped a firm hand against his gun and accompanying claps came from the other men.

'There is another choice,' Carter said. He grabbed his hat and swung it on his head. 'When Lee and me were in Silver Creek, Marshal Brown deputized us. We got a right to enforce the law now.'

Lorne nodded. 'Enforce away.'

'I intend to.' Carter drew himself to his full height. 'Lorne Wayne, you is under arrest.'

'What?' Lorne snapped.

Stem and the other ranch hands swirled round to glare up at Carter, but Carter stood tall.

'Four months ago, twenty-seven miners died in the Silver Gulch mine, and I reckon you had something to do with it.'

'Abe killed them.' Lorne held his arms wide. 'I told you that.'

'But he might not have acted on his own. Someone might have ordered him to bring down that tunnel.'

'Abe brought down that tunnel to force us to pay his twenty per cent.' Lorne sneered. 'So why in tarnation are you arresting me?'

'Because that might not be the full story. You might have told Abe to do it to end the pay dispute. And I reckon the only way we can sort this out is if I arrest you, then let proper justice take its course, which will be fairer than the justice you'll get at the end of Abe's gun.'

For long moments Lorne stared at Carter. Then he snorted.

'Either join us in facing Abe, or stand aside and let me see how I can get us out of this alive.'

Carter patted his gunbelt. 'I'm arresting you one way or another.'

Lorne glanced at Lee. 'Guess you're with Carter?'

'Yup,' Lee said, slotting a thumb into his gunbelt.

Lorne glanced at Stem. 'And your view on this?'

Stem folded his arms. He lowered his head a moment, then nodded.

'Carter's right. You wanted to end that pay dispute, and the tunnel collapsing did end it. I don't know whether Abe brought it down to force you to pay him more, or you ordered him to bring it down to end the dispute. But if you're under suspicion of having given Abe that order, you should be in the custody of a lawman. And Carter and Lee are the nearest we got to the law around here.'

Lorne waved his hands above his head, his eyes wide and hurt.

'You knew me even before Alistair and me found the mine. How could you reckon I ordered Abe to do something so terrible?'

'I reckon that. . .' Stem sighed and ran a hand through his hair. 'I don't reckon it was you. If anyone gave that order, it was Alistair.'

'Thank you.' Lorne turned to Carter. 'I still reckon Abe killed those miners as a warning, but Alistair and me had different ideas about how to end the pay dispute, and bringing down a tunnel ain't far off some of the ideas he had. So it *could* have been him.'

'If that's true,' Carter said, taking a long pace towards Lorne, 'you'll get the chance to tell your story. I'll take you to Silver Creek and get the proper authorities to work out just what happened.'

Lorne snorted. 'It's a fine sentiment, but the second I set foot outside that door, I'll be spitting bullets.'

'Lee and I will protect you.'

Lorne rubbed his chin, then with a sly grin, he nodded.

'All right. I'll let you arrest me. But you two can walk out the door first. I'll follow you out.'

For long moments, Lee and Carter looked at each other. Then both men shared a nod.

Lee gestured for Lorne to surrender his gun to Stem. Then, with Carter leading and Lee a pace behind, they strode to the door and went outside.

A pace out from the doorway, they faced the cart.

'Abe,' Carter shouted, 'I've arrested Lorne.'

'You ain't a lawman,' Abe shouted from behind the cart.

Carter shrugged. 'I might not be, but I intend to do the right thing. Whatever your intentions are towards the ownership of the mine, they ain't important now. We'll sort this out the right way.'

'I got no desire to kill a miner,' Abe roared. 'But don't push me. You're in no position to make demands of me.'

Lorne edged outside to stand behind Lee, but Lee strode forward a pace to stand beside Carter, forcing Lorne to sidle up behind the larger man.

'We ain't demanding,' Lee shouted. 'We just want to right wrongs – as you do.'

'Then stand aside. I'm removing Lorne for your benefit, too.'

Lee raised his hands from his holster and sauntered along the side of the house towards the cart as Carter and Lorne edged in the other direction.

'I ain't interested in benefiting from your actions. I walked out of the mine yesterday and not even your promises of a share in the mine can make me return.' Lee rolled his shoulders. 'Carter and me are deputies now.'

Abe chuckled. 'So, you ain't a miner no more?'

'Nope.'

Lee winced, then Abe's gunfire blasted into the wall behind him. In desperate self-preservation, he dashed for cover with Carter and Lorne a scant two paces ahead of him. They hurled themselves behind the nearest cover, an overturned fence, and rolled round to lie behind it.

Lee and Carter blasted off a round of gunfire, then lay flat.

'You're an idiot,' Carter whispered to Lee.

'I know,' Lee muttered. 'I just removed the only advantage we had.'

More gunfire ripped into the fence.

Lee waited for a lull, then slammed his gun on the fence and blasted at the cart.

From the house, gunfire ripped from each window as the ranch hands maintained continuous fire, but then Lee realized that some of the lead was hurtling over his shoulder from behind them.

Lee pushed Carter flat, slammed Lorne's head down, then peered over his shoulder.

Brady, Talbot and Walter were galloping into the ranch grounds.

A ragged cheer sounded from the house as the three men dismounted and leapt behind a wrecked coach. Within seconds, they'd slammed their guns on the top of the coach and were blasting at Abe's position.

Lee and Carter waved their thanks to the small, belated, but still welcome posse and settled down on their bellies with their guns resting on the top of the fence.

Now with gunfire coming from three different directions, Abe, Elliott and Orem were trapped. Every time they edged above their cart, lead ripped into the woodwork, pinning them down.

For ten minutes of sporadic gunfire the stand-off continued, before irritation got the better of Orem. He jumped to his feet and sprayed an arc of gunfire at the fence, but a clean shot from Brady slammed into his guts. He staggered back and around to fold over the side of the cart and lie with his arms dangling.

With their numbers having been depleted, Abe and Elliott no longer returned fire and decided to stay down.

Five minutes into this lull, Carter cleared his throat.

'Abe,' he shouted, 'we got you pinned down.'

'That's your mistake,' Abe roared.

'Quit the threats. All you're facing today is your own death. Throw your guns out and we can end this.'

'You don't scare me. I know where you all are, and you're nowhere near sneaky enough. I ain't surrendering.'

'And I ain't asking you to. You killed Alistair Marriott and Marshal Brown, but from the sound of it, there was plenty of mutual feuding between you, so I got no reason to arrest you about those killings.

And as I have no information on any other wrongs you've done, I'll let you leave. But only if you throw in your guns now.'

'And what about Lorne?'

'Lorne will provide the truth about what happened at the mine. I'll see to that.'

'Lorne must die.'

'And if he's guilty of anything, he will swing, but you ain't the one deciding that.'

Behind the cart, subdued muttering between Abe and Elliott could be heard, then Abe chuckled.

'All right. I'll throw out my guns, but only after Lorne has agreed to my contract.'

Lorne furrowed his brow and glanced at Carter, but Lee shuffled on his belly to Lorne's side.

'Abe wants you to relinquish all rights to the mine,' he whispered. 'He intends to hand over ownership to the miners.'

As Lorne's mouth fell open, Carter raised his head above the fence.

'Abe, throw out your contract and Lorne will read it.'

The contract was thrown from behind the cart and landed just before the fence.

With his gun held out before him, Carter jumped to his feet and scurried from the fence. He grabbed the contract, then vaulted the fence and dropped on his front beside Lorne.

Lorne read the contract. A smile emerged as he read the final clause.

'There are hundreds of them. That'll never. . .' Lorne glanced around at the crumbling fences, the rotting carts, the derelict buildings. He shrugged. 'Suppose my life started collapsing the moment we found that silver load. I was born to be a rancher, and perhaps it's time to return to that life and sort out this place.'

Lorne handed the contract to Carter, and Carter hurled the contract into the clear space before the cart.

'Lorne has agreed your contract. Now throw out your guns.'

A gun flew from behind the cart, hurtling end over end. Abe's second gun joined it a moment later.

More muttering could be heard from behind the cart, followed by a barked order. Then Elliott threw out his gun, which landed beside Abe's guns.

With a last glance at each other, Carter and Lee stood, then Lorne. But Lorne glanced at the cart repeatedly.

Abe and Elliott stood, and with a series of nods to each other, everyone paced into the clear space before the house.

One by one, Stem and the ranch hands emerged from the house. Stem glared at Elliott, but then strode to face Brady and the others who remained of Marriott's ranch hands. He patted Brady's shoulder and received a solid slap on the back in return.

A ripple of nodding and smiling passed between the men from both ranches.

'Seems like this is over,' Abe said, folding his vast arms. 'The mine is in the hands of the people who deserve the profits, and justice will decide who is to blame for causing the mine massacre.'

'Justice will happen,' Carter said.

Abe crouched and pointed a wide finger at Carter.

'But you'd better deliver it, or I'll return and ensure it does happen.'

Carter gulped, but then stood tall and faced Abe.

'Justice *will* happen, but whatever the result is, it'll happen the right way.'

'It won't,' a weak voice cried out.

Everyone turned to see a man stagger through the ranch gates. He was in rags, his tattered clothing encrusted with dried and fresh blood and dangling from a haggard frame that was torn and shredded.

'Alistair Marriott,' Lorne whispered.

CHAPTER 19

Alistair Marriott tottered another step, then fell to his knees.

'Lorne,' he muttered, 'forget justice. Only we two can sort this out.'

Lorne backed a long pace to stand beside Carter.

'I'm in Deputy Lyle's custody. We'll let justice take its course.'

'We can't do that.' Alistair wiped a red-streaked arm over his equally bloodied brow. 'You and I both know it was your decision for Abe to bring down the tunnel.'

Lee stood before Lorne.

'He didn't,' Lee shouted. 'It was your decision.'

'Is that what Lorne said?' Alistair snorted and kneaded his bloodshot eyes with a shaking hand. 'That man always was a liar.'

For a long while, Lee stared at Alistair, but through red-rimmed eyes Alistair met his gaze with an equally firm one. He turned to Lorne.

'This true, Lorne?' Lee demanded.

Lorne glared at Lee, but then his eyes flashed with the hint of something that Lee had seen in his eyes when they first met. Back then, Lee had thought it was surprise, but now he wondered if it was guilt.

Lorne lowered his head. A short sob escaped his lips. Then he looked up, a wetness gleaming in his eyes.

'I can't lie to you any more. The collapsed tunnel had nothing to do with Abe's demands for more money. Marriott gave Abe that order and I didn't oppose him.' Lorne held his arms wide. 'But believe this – I agreed that Abe should bring down an *unoccupied* tunnel. But I reckon that didn't satisfy Alistair, and so he ensured that the miners were in the tunnel.'

'That's a lie,' Alistair murmured from the ground, his voice weak.

Lee glanced back and forth between Alistair and Lorne, trying to gauge which one of them was telling the truth purely from their postures, but as both men hung their heads, he lowered his, too.

Carter paced between the two ranchers. He patted Lee's shoulder, then backed away until he had both men in his sights.

'We can't decide who's telling the truth now. I'll arrest you both and we'll work out who is to blame when—'

'We won't,' Alistair muttered, his voice weakening by the moment. 'It'll be the word of one man against the word of another man. So, we have to sort this out another way – Abe's way – the way we should have settled our feuding long ago.'

Alistair slipped his gun from his belt and edged it up to point the shaking weapon at Lorne.

Lorne raised his hands. 'Shooting me won't prove who was responsible.'

'It won't.' Alistair rolled on to his haunches, then staggered to his feet. 'But whichever one of us is still alive in one minute can tell their story, and there ain't anyone who can disprove what they'll say.'

'We ain't gunslingers.'

'We ain't. But . . .'

Alistair tried to slot his gun into its holster, but his hand was shaking so much and the blood that had dribbled from his tortured body had slicked the holster, so the barrel slid down the leather. He grabbed his arm and levered it up to rest it on his other arm, instead.

Lorne nodded. 'I know. We just hire gunslingers to kill for us.'

'But now it's time to take responsibility for what we did in Silver Gulch.'

Lorne glared at Alistair for a long moment, but as Alistair swayed back and forth, then stumbled to his knees, he nodded. With his eyebrows raised, he glanced at Carter.

Carter rubbed his brow, then raised his hands and glanced at Lee.

Lee sighed, looking at each rancher in turn. He shook his head.

'There's been enough killing in Silver Gulch,' he said. 'It ends now with proper justice for the murdered miners.'

A thud sounded behind Lee and he swirled round to see that Abe had hurled himself at his guns and now clutched them in the two great hams of his hands. Lying on his side, Abe aimed the guns up at Lee and chuckled.

'These two have to end this, and that will be proper justice.'

Lee glared at Abe, but as Alistair and Lorne grunted their approval, he snorted his contempt for them all and backed to stand beside Carter.

Abe rolled to his feet and underhanded a gun to Lorne's feet.

Lorne grabbed the gun and slotted it into his belt. He rolled his shoulders and faced Alistair.

On the ground, Alistair took deep breaths, then slammed his forehead to the dirt and levered himself back on to his haunches. He stood. Still he swayed. Blood continued to ooze from his battered body.

'You ready?' he whispered, holding his gun in a shaking hand and aiming it in the vague direction of Lorne.

Lorne licked his lips and widened his eyes, his stance more assured than Lee had seen before.

'Yup. Just holster your gun and we can get to it.'

'If you insist.' Alistair glanced at his gun, then turned it on Lorne and blasted a bullet into his shoulder.

Lorne spun back and fell to the ground, clutching his shoulder. As he writhed, Alistair staggered forward to loom over him.

'You said we'd fight this out fairly,' Lorne said between gasps.

'I did. But I lied. I just wanted to see that hope in your eyes that you might live through this.'

Alistair ripped a bullet through Lorne's throat,

then threw the gun aside and staggered round to face Carter, a grim smile on his face.

'Got to arrest you now,' Carter said. 'And I *will* find out the truth about what happened in the Silver Gulch mine.'

Alistair sneered, then fell forward, but he threw out a leg and stopped himself tumbling to the ground.

'The only truth that matters is that twenty-seven miners died. The rest is just rich dead men squabbling over silver they never mined.'

'I ain't satisfied with—'

'And neither am I,' Lee muttered, pushing Carter aside. He drew his gun and aimed it at Alistair. 'That shooting proved nothing. I have to know the truth. Which one of you two is responsible?'

Alistair stared down the barrel of Lee's gun. His jaw slackened. His eyes rolled back into his head and he fell to his knees, then keeled over on to his front.

Lee dashed to Alistair's side. He dropped to his knees and threw Alistair on his back.

'Let me sleep,' Alistair murmured, his voice hollow, his eyes closing.

'You ain't going until you tell me who ordered those miners into the tunnel.' Lee prised open Alistair's eyes, but saw only the whites.

Alistair chuckled, the hollow sound grating and ripping from deep inside his tortured body.

'It wasn't me.'

'Then Lorne?'

In a last feeble gesture, Alistair shrugged from Lee's grip.

'You're acting the lawman.' Alistair lay back, his breathing ragged and shallow, his voice fainter than the wind. 'You figure it out.'

Lee shook Alistair's shoulders, but Alistair's head lolled back and forth. Spit dribbled from his slack mouth.

Carter knelt beside Lee and prised his hands away from Alistair.

'He's dead,' Carter said. 'He ain't talking no more. This is over.'

'It ain't over until I know who killed the miners.' Lee glared up at Carter. 'And how will I ever find that out?'

'Like he said. You're a lawman now, and so am I.' Carter patted Lee's shoulder. 'We'll figure it out.'

CHAPTER 20

Abe Mountain sauntered over to the dead men. With the toe of his boot, he rocked Alistair's head from side to side, then did the same to Lorne. He chuckled, then turned to glare down at Carter.

'You sticking with your promise not to arrest me?'

Carter blew out his cheeks. 'Don't know much about the law, but I reckon justice was done here. And whatever you've done over the last day had some form of justification.'

Carter glanced at Lee, who nodded.

Abe tipped his hat. 'Then you can live.'

Abe swaggered around Carter to his horse. With surprising grace, he leapt on to his steed and swung it round.

'Where are you going?' Carter asked.

'I've got a contract to file in Bear Rock.' Abe stared across the rock-strewn ground ahead. 'And I've amassed some other debts over the years. Now I got into the habit of righting wrongs, I might right me a few more.'

Carter nodded and with a final nod down to Lee,

Abe headed for the ranch gates.

Elliott glanced back at Stem and the other ranch hands. He snorted and sauntered to his horse.

Lee turned and strode back to the house with Carter, but a stray thought battered at his mind and so he turned back, pacing up to Elliott. As Elliott lifted a leg to mount his horse, he slammed a hand on his arm.

'You going with Abe?' he asked.

Elliott glanced at the arm and sneered.

'It ain't your concern, but I am.' Elliott lowered his leg and squared off to Lee. 'Why are you interested in my business?'

'You were a mine supervisor before you were a ranch boss. You hoping to do either again?'

'I might.' Elliott raised his leg to the stirrup. 'It depends on what Abe does next.'

Lee shrugged. 'But why are you staying with Abe? He doesn't own the mine now.'

'Yes, he does. Alistair and the others are dead. And everyone who's with Abe gets an equal share.'

'And that equal share includes a few hundred miners, too.' Lee raised his eyebrows.

'What?' Elliott slammed his leg to the ground, his eyes blazing.

Lee just smiled and folded his arms. 'Your share of Abe's venture won't be much – unlike the share you used to get from him, and from Alistair.'

'What you getting at?'

'I'm wondering why the meanest supervisor I ever knew left the mine to become Marriott's ranch boss just after the mining disaster.'

Elliott breathed heavily, then lunged for his gun, but Lee grabbed his arm. Elliott ripped his arm away and thrust his elbow into Lee's guts, knocking him to the ground.

As Lee floundered, Elliott leapt on his horse.

'What you doing, Lee?' Carter shouted, running towards him.

'I figured it out,' Lee cried from the ground. 'Elliott was a mine supervisor, and he was the only one who could order miners to be in that tunnel when Abe brought it down.'

Elliott snorted and galloped for the ranch gates, but then he pulled hard on the reins, swung his horse around, and galloped straight at Lee.

Lee scrambled on his hands and feet to the side, then hurled himself flat and rolled. Pounding hoofs blasted inches from his head.

Elliott dragged his horse to a halt and bore down on Lee again, but from the side Carter took a long run and hurled himself at Elliott and, in a clawing swipe, pulled him from his galloping horse.

The two men landed in a heap and tumbled over each other, but Elliott bundled Carter on to his back, then slugged his fist straight down on his throat.

Carter croaked and, with a desperate protective lunge, threw his hands to his own throat.

Elliott pulled his fist back, ready to slam it down on the prone Carter again, but then he leapt to his feet and ripped out his gun. He set his feet on either side of Carter's chest and aimed the gun down at Carter's head.

But then Elliott's arms shot up as Stem grabbed

him in a bear hug from behind.

Elliott struggled and kicked, but Stem set his feet wide and wrapped his arms even tighter around him. Then, with Elliott's arms held high above his head in a firm grip, Stem walked him away from Carter.

Lee rolled to his feet and dashed to Stem's side. On tiptoe he prised the gun from Elliott's hand, then stood back to face Elliott.

Elliott muttered oaths and struggled, but Stem tightened his grip so hard that Lee was sure he heard bones creaking.

'He ain't going anywhere,' Stem said, chuckling.

Lee shook his head. 'He is. And I'd be obliged if you'd help me and Carter take him back to Silver Creek.'

'I'll help.' Stem smiled. 'But only if you let me do one thing first.'

'What's that?'

Stem chuckled, then lowered Elliott's arms to his sides. He flexed his shoulders, then spun the man round.

As Elliott tottered back a step, Stem rocked back his fist and slugged the man's jaw with a sharp uppercut that snapped his head back, then he smashed his cheek with a round-armed slug that pummelled his opponent to the ground

Even as Elliott was sliding to a halt, Stem was on him and bundling him over on to his front. He looked up at the ranch hands, receiving a huge wave of cheering from everyone, including Talbot, Walter and Brady, then he slammed Elliott's face into the dirt.

He ground the face back and forth, then lifted it by the hair. With a huge grin, he lowered his head to glance at Elliott's features.

Elliott blinked the dirt from his eyes. He mouthed an oath at Stem, but his mouth was cut and distorted and the words emerged garbled.

Stem shrugged and ground Elliott's face in the dirt a second time, then lifted his head and ground him down a third time.

Sporting a huge smile, Stem released his grip on Elliott's head. He knelt on his back and batted his hands free of dust.

'I reckon grinding Elliott's face into the dirt three times has satisfied me. I can help you take him now.'

Lee patted Stem's shoulder, then dragged Carter to his feet. Carter stood hunched a moment, then coughed several times and claimed to be feeling fine.

As Carter and Lee judged that the problems caused by Alistair and Lorne's feuding had ended, they told the men from the two ranches to deal with the bodies, while Stem trussed Elliott up.

With Elliott safely strapped over the back of his horse, Stem barked additional orders to the ranch hands to start cleaning up the ranch.

Stem even ordered Talbot, Walter and Brady to head back to their ranch and resume their duties.

And to Lee's surprise, they tipped their hats to Stem and rode off towards the Marriott ranch.

Then, while the remaining ranch hands scurried to their allocated tasks, the three men mounted their horses and headed to the gates with Elliott in tow.

At the ranch gates, they halted a moment and

watched Abe's dwindling form head down the trail, then they started their journey back to Silver Creek.

Lee turned to Stem. 'You were giving everyone orders back there, but ain't you out of a job now?'

'Someone will want this ranch. I reckon if we clean it up, it'll attract plenty of interest, and perhaps even more than the Marriott ranch.' Stem grinned. 'The Wayne ranch always was the best.'

'You do that. It's better than hanging around the trading post.'

Stem licked his lips, then shrugged. 'I reckon you're right. And are you two returning after we've dealt with Elliott? I reckon you've impressed me enough to be on full pay.'

'Nope,' Lee said, as Carter grunted his approval. 'We're lawmen now.'

Stem glanced at Carter, then at Lee.

'Which one of you reckons he's the deputy and which one reckons he's the town marshal?'

'I am,' Lee and Carter said together.

They glanced at each other, then Lee shrugged.

'Perhaps Silver Creek ain't ready for a Chinese town marshal just yet. If either of us gets the job, Carter should be the marshal.'

'Obliged.' Carter tipped his hat, then faced the front.

'With me as your deputy, of course.'

Carter glanced at Stem and winked. 'If you want the job, Lee, you'll have to apply.'

'Hey,' Lee shouted. Then he noticed that Carter and Stem were smiling. He laughed and hurried on ahead. 'I'll think about it.'